ETERNITY

Jenna Kay Pridgen

First Edition 2013

The characters, events, and locales portrayed in this book are fictitious. Any similarity to real persons, living or dead, is coincidental and not intended by the author.

ISBN: 0988298260
ISBN-13: 978-0-9882982-6-2

LIFELINE Press
Gainesville, Georgia
Printed in the United States of America

All who are victorious will inherit all these blessings, and I will be their God, and they will be my children. But cowards, unbelievers, the corrupt, murderers, the immoral, those who practice witchcraft, idol worshipers, and all liars – their fate is in the fiery lake of burning sulfur.

This is the second death.

Revelation 21:7-8

ETERNITY

- Story 1-

Jenna Kay Pridgen

Chapter 1

Jeff

The wait was the hardest part of all. The tapping of pens and the murmuring of voices were the only noises in the courtroom as we wait for the jury to come back with their verdict. My client, Billy Fitz, fidgeted in the seat next to me. He was sweating bullets, and for a good reason. Child molestation did not go unpunished, and with his filthy track record his mind was telling him that he would be going away for a long time.

Billy had ruined six little female lives – six that the public knew about, that is. The odds were stacked against us. Everyone in the room wanted him thrown in jail for life or dead. Luckily, Billy has me, Jeff Craner, Defense Attorney for the slime balls that inhabit the city.

Drumming my fingers against the glossy wooden table, I run the case through my brain one more time. The Prosecution's case had been extremely weak, giving my client and I a little bit of an edge. Hardly any evidence, only the parent's of the young girls, whose ages ranged from five to thirteen. With no eyewitnesses or DNA samples, the case was an easy one. Even with the high-profile status of the case (being on public television), I'd not broken a sweat or stumbled over any words. Sure, I knew Billy was guilty, and what he'd done was unforgivable, but in this business you need concrete evidence to bring down the villain.

Yes, I said it. This was just business. That's all it was to me. I'd worked hard to get where I am today, and I had no intentions on slowing down. Possessions cost money, like my Mercedes and high-rise apartment. If I had to prove every criminal innocent to keep the money rolling in, that's what I'd do. The one and only reason I'd become a lawyer was to gain wealth, not to actually help mankind. No, mankind was way more corrupt and volatile than little 'ol me could ever be. I wasn't selfish ... I was a realist. And frankly, I felt above everyone else, including the stoic judge.

Truth is, money makes the world go round, and if I was to win this case, I'd be set for life. Also, if I win this case, a celebration would commence tonight. Dinner, some wine, and my girlfriend for the past year, Serena Little.

A smile touched my lips as the image of sweet, reliable, honest Serena flashed through my mind. I'd met her downtown at a small coffee shop. She'd been coming out of the shop as I was coming in. Her coffee had splashed all over my expensive Ralph Lauren suit.

At first I'd been ready to tell this klutz of a person off, but when my gaze caught hold of her baby blues, my frozen heart had completed melted. She was the prettiest woman I'd ever seen, with her petite build and a sundress that clung to her sultry curves. Her long dark hair had been pulled into a loose ponytail. By Hollywood's standards, she was overweight, wearing a size twelve. But to me she was perfect.

"Oh my gosh, I'm so sorry!" she'd reacted, quickly taking her napkins and dabbing at the coffee staining my chest. I'd smiled, watching her go in a frenzy over the coffee spilled all over me. If it had been anyone else, I'd have ripped into them like a shark, but not her. She was an angel.

"Stop," I'd told her, snatching her hand. A gasp slid from her lips as her eyes locked with mine.

Again she'd said, "I'm so sorry."

I'd shook my head. "I'm not." She'd tilted her head in confusion, so I made my move. "My name's Jeff Craner. What's yours?" She'd realized I wasn't angry and gave me the first smile of many that would follow.

From that moment on we'd been together. I'd found out she was a school teacher at a local church, and lived in a tiny apartment a few blocks away from mine. She loved kids and wanted two whenever she found her soul mate. And I believed that I was the one she'd been waiting for.

Serena was everything I wanted in a woman – beautiful, honest, giving, nurturing. The only problem, and the problem that we fought over daily, was her beliefs. She was a devout Christian, a *Jesus Freak* to some extent. She was always on me about going to church and getting saved, like she could ever change me. With my charm and gifts, though, I was able to sustain her, getting her mind off me and concentrating on herself. But usually the next day she'd be on my case about getting right with God.

Personally, I didn't believe in God, Heaven, or Hell. I'd been raised in an atheist home, which meant I was to believe in myself, and that if I wanted success I'd have to earn it. Depending on a fabricated God was a waste of time, and my parents believed the same way. My father was a lawyer in the south, making him a very prominent figure in the area. My mother was the perfect mother, taking care of her husband like a wife should. I'd grown up in a mansion, with maids and nannies, while my parents took luxurious vacations, living the high life.

That's how I saw Serena and I, married with a couple of kids, living a glamorous life, and believing in each other, rather than believing in a fictional God. Whether I won the case or not, I was asking her to marry me tonight. I'd promise her a life of wealth and security. She'd be able to quit her low-paying job and live in a beautiful home, where maids took care of everything. Maybe then she'd give up on religion and come down to planet earth. Maybe then she'd stop trying to change me, and accept me for who I was and not for who I wasn't.

However, I did have some changing to do if I was to marry Serena. We'd been together for a year and she'd been faithful the whole time. Unfortunately, I had not.

Throughout the year I'd been on the road, having nightly visits from numerous call girls. Women were my number one weakness. At the time I didn't see anything wrong with their visits, and honestly, I still felt that way. After all, I knew my father had a few women he could call up when he was stuck on the road. Mother never knew, and I had all of my father's instincts. It was casual sex, nothing more, and as long as I was careful, what difference did it make? No harm, no foul.

Things may have been different if Serena weren't so religious. It had been a year, and we still hadn't had sex. She'd made a promise to her made-up God, promising that she'd wait until she married the one meant for her. To me, that was a bunch of silly, nonsensical garbage. My hopes for the evening was that she would change her mind about her stupid promise. The two-karat platinum diamond ring would most likely alter her religious thinking.

Reality came crashing down when the twelve jurors walked in. Chairs scraped against the hardwood floors as the jurors took their seats. A hush around the room followed, no one speaking. Everyone was anxious to hear the verdict. My heart pounded in my chest when the judge told us to stand. Child molester Billy was shaking like a leaf.

"How does the jury find the defendant?" the judge inquired, narrowing his eyes at the juror standing.

The juror, an older gentleman, announced, "We the jury find the defendant, Billy Fitz ... not guilty."

Angry shouts filled the courtroom, but I hardly heard them. Billy took my hand in his sweaty one, shaking it vigorously and thanking me at the same time. I said something, but I couldn't tell you what. I was on cloud nine, my happiness soaring to new heights. The only thought that cruised through my brain was the big fat check I was about to receive, and that Serena was going to be a very happy woman.

The Usher

Hidden in my dark shadows, I listened to the courtroom's reaction to the verdict. Shouts of confusion and displeasure filtered through the air – oh, how I loved all this commotion! It was music to my dreadful ears. I zeroed in on Mr. Craner, the man who had proved Billy Fitz innocent. Little did that puny nothing know that I, along with a few of my minions, had been the ones to persuade the weak-minded jury that there wasn't enough evidence in the case. Like sheep to the slaughter, they'd bought it, and now Billy could prowl the streets, hunting for new prey.

I sat back, twiddling my thumbs. No human eye could see me. I was invisible within my dark shadow as I continued to observe this Mr. Craner. The smile on his face shown of arrogance and pride; his black heart was filled to the brim with lustful desires and lies.

All around the room Holy Ones were scattered about, using their Father's grace to comfort those who had been hurt and confused by the jury's verdict. There was even a couple of them surrounding Mr. Craner and his client, attempting to break through their evil consciences, but the barrier was thick with corruption. The two had no sense of shame or morals. Pride, lust, greed, and power were their gods, leaving them blind to the pain and sorrow around them.

It wouldn't be long now. I could feel the storm brewing in the not-so-far distance. The high Mr. Craner was on would not last long. He, like many before him, would eventually fall, and I would be waiting.

Yes. I would be waiting.

Chapter 2

Serena

As soon as the bell rang, my students jumped from their seats, ready for a weekend away from school. I watched them from my desk, smiling as they talked and laughed with one another. So happy, so free, not having a care in the world.

A lot of days I wished I could feel that way again.

"Miss Serena?" a small voice said, breaking me out of my wondering thoughts. Turning my head, I saw it was little Tucker. He stared at me with huge brown eyes.

"Yes, Tucker?" I responded, leaning across the desk to ruffle his dirty blonde hair.

He grinned, showing off his missing two front teeth. "Hope you have a good weekend."

"Aw," I cooed, my hand raising to my chest. "I hope you have a good one, too." He grinned one more time, then shuffled out the door with his tennis shoes untied.

My job to some would be considered boring, maybe even tedious, but I loved it. I loved the joyous atmosphere, the enthusiastic kids in my class, and my co-workers. It was truly a blessing to make money at a job I loved. It wasn't much money, but seeing the smiles on the faces of happy children was a reward in itself.

Glancing around the small classroom, I released a loud sigh. I was ready for the weekend, but not looking forward to it. Something had been weighing on my heart and it was time to lift it off. Tonight I was doing something that would change and alter my life, placing it back on the right path.

I was breaking up with Jeff.

Tears gathered in my eyes as an image of his blonde hair and smiling face paddled through my mind. His dark green eyes and contagious grin had hooked me that day I'd walked out of the coffee shop. When we'd sat down and talked for hours I thought that God finally blessed me with the man I was to marry. Though after a year of being together, a realization smacked me across the face.

Jeff and I were not right for each other.

I thought I'd hit the jackpot with Jeff, which was my first mistake. A young lawyer interested in a underpaid school teacher like myself? Well, that was true. He was interested in me. Very interested. That still didn't change the fact that he wasn't a believer in God, or that he didn't believe Heaven and Hell actually existed. He'd been raised in a home with dysfunctional parents who worshiped money and spent it in heavy doses. His father, a lawyer like him, was very successful in deceiving the courts and paying people to testify in his cases. Jeff had grown up with parents who never taught him the importance of morals and values. They never taught him about God and the love of Jesus Christ.

Our relationship had been doomed from the beginning. I realized that now. No matter how hard I tried to help him, I was always let down by the knowledge that he wasn't going to change. Whenever I invited him to church, he'd shrug it off and call me a Jesus Freak. Then he'd laugh, saying he was just joking. I'd let it go, hoping that time would bend and shape his troubled heart. I thought I could steer him closer to God, and I prayed daily that he would let go of his impervious pride. Deep down in my heart, I knew that day would never come. Not with my help, anyway.

In the beginning of the relationship he'd been very caring, showering me with flowers and gifts. Though the last couple of months he'd been showing male chauvinist qualities. He would snap at me for the smallest things, then apologize later with roses and dinner. I was a strong-willed woman and was taught to never let anyone (especially men) talk to me like I was nothing, but the love I had for him had blinded me ... That is, until I found a napkin with a woman's name and number on it, which had been kissed with the brightest red lipstick I'd ever seen. I tried telling myself that it wasn't what I thought. That it wasn't what it looked like. Jeff wouldn't cheat on me ... *would* he?

After I'd found that disturbing napkin, I'd gone over to his high-rise and searched through his belongings. He'd given me a key and told me I could stay there when he was on the road, telling me that anything he owned, I owned. At first I felt guilty going through his things, but then I'd take a peek at the incriminating piece of tissue and get fired up again.

Eventually I gave up, not finding anything in his apartment that would make me think he was cheating. I'd been about to leave when his computer caught my eye. Deciding to take a gander, I turned it on, logged on with his information ... and became completely crushed.

In one sitting I'd found about twenty women he kept in

contact with when he was on the road. Apparently when he went on "business trips" he'd have nightly visits with these women. Finding his credit card statement, I also determined that he wined and dined them before heading to five star hotels. A few of the rooms were actually categorized as "Honeymoon Suites".

The night I'd gotten this information, I'd gone to my apartment and cried my eyes out. Crying out to God, asking for His guidance and will in this situation. The next morning I got my answer. It was time to let Jeff go. Despite it all, I loved Jeff. I wanted him to change for the better, but I knew we couldn't stay together. I knew that if he didn't change he'd go to Hell. I didn't want anyone I knew to go to Hell. Hopefully someone would come along and help him see the light.

"Are you going to stay here all day or what?" Rose, my assistant, inquired. She picked up supplies from the tables and placed them in one of the many small cubicles that lined the walls.

Quickly, I dabbed at a stray tear sliding down my cheek. "Um ... no, I was about to get going."

"Hey," Rose said, placing a hand on my shoulder. "You're crying. What's wrong?"

With that one single question, I dived into the whole story about what I'd found out about Jeff, crying the entire time. She listened while I explained my feelings and what I was going to do later that night. By the end of the story, she had tears forming in her own eyes, hating to see me in so much pain.

A few moments of hugging went by before Rose told me, "You're doing the right thing, Serena. You've been with him for so long and you've tried to help him. But he's not right for you. And he's never going to change."

"The sad thing is," I began, biting back a sob, "I love him. I know that I shouldn't, but I can't help but ... *feel* for him."

Rose nodded. "Most likely you'll always have a tiny part of your heart loving him, but truthfully, if he can do that to you, he doesn't truly love you."

"It was doomed from the beginning." I blew my nose. "Why did God send him my direction? I just don't get it."

She shrugged. "Maybe God sent him your way so that he could be changed. But that's when freewill comes into play. Jeff has chosen not to change. All you can do now is pray for him. Let God work on him."

"True," I agreed, adding, "Though there's no way I can be with him."

Rose concurred. "I think you're doing the right thing.

Especially since he just helped that child molester get off scot free."

My breath hitched in my throat, my stomach feeling like someone had just punched it. I knew he was defending Billy Fitz, but had no idea that he'd win the case. I was sure when he took the case that he'd see this man as a danger to young children and want to put him behind bars.

"He ... He won the case?" I wondered out loud, still dismayed by the news.

Rose frowned. "Yes, Serena, he did. The jury found Billy Fitz not guilty due to lack of evidence. And talk is going around that Jeff may land a huge gig at a firm in California." A sad look crossed her face. "He made a lot of money on this case."

"For what?" I jumped up, knocking my seat to the ground. Anger had me curled in its firm grip. "So this Billy Fitz can go out wherever he wants and pick another child to destroy? A couple of the little girls were only five years old! The same age as our..." I halted my words, taking in all the empty desks in the classroom. Slowly I picked up my chair and plopped down in it, putting my head on my desk. A few silent moments ticked by before Rose gave my shoulder a squeeze.

"I'm going home," she told me softly. "But if you need me

tonight, give me a call and I'll be right over. You're not alone, Serena. You're going to be okay."

Without lifting my head I whispered, "I know. I'll call you later."

I heard Rose's footsteps clap out of the classroom, then the door clicked shut. The only sounds in the classroom was the thrumming of the air conditioning and my slight sobbing.

How could he do this? How could he defend a man so evil, so bent on the destruction of little lives? A man that, no doubt in my mind, was covered with demons. Then again, Jeff had a few demons of his own.

My cell phone vibrated, alerting me that I had a voice message. The message was from Jeff. I clicked the message button and put it on speaker. With rattled nerves, I listened to his voice coming through the phone.

Hey babe! I want to meet you at that fancy french restaurant you like so much! Say, around seven-thirty? I'll be waiting — oh, and be sure to dress up. I've got a little surprise for you. Love you.

The message beeped off. I stared at my phone for a long while, thinking about what I would say to him tonight. At the moment I couldn't form the right thoughts. I was mad and terrified at the same time. With conflicting thoughts sprinting at each other in my mind, there was only one thing I could do.

I prayed.

The Messenger

Serena Little was praying for wisdom, for the right words to say to Jeff Craner. Her relationship with the lawyer had been in a downward spiral for the last few months. She'd been wrong in the beginning, thinking that she could change such an evil, deceitful man, even with her intentions being entirely sincere. Only God can change a man's heart, but the man has to be willing.

Jeff was not a willing man.

When she was a little girl, she always tried to find the good in everyone. That had led her to many broken hearts and hurt feelings. Fortunately, she was stronger than most girls, because she relied on the Father to free her from the many hurts she'd suffered.

Serena had grown into a strong woman, still holding firm in her beliefs. Even now, through the tears she was busy shedding, she asked for God's intervention in this dire situation.

She loved this man, but they weren't meant to be together. They were too different, and plus, Jeff wasn't her soul mate – the one she would marry lived on the other side of the city.

"God, please," Serena sobbed, raising her hands in the air. "Help me."

I smiled and walked over to her. She couldn't see me. I was an angel of light, a messenger to God's children. I placed a consoling hand on her shoulder. She couldn't feel my hand, but a comfort like no other flowed through me to her – God's mercy, grace, love, and comfort.

Whispering in her ear I said, "Follow the Holy Spirit."

Almost immediately, she quit crying as a knowing look crossed her face.

"Thank you, Lord," she said softly. She grabbed her pocketbook and left the room.

I grinned, lifting my gaze to the ceiling. "She's going to be alright, Father. She's going to be alright."

Chapter 3

Jeff

Tonight was going to be perfect. I'd reserved a table in the very back of the restaurant, requesting that candlelight be our only fixture. A bottle of champagne with two glasses filled halfway sat on the small round table. Soft violin music played in the background, giving off a romantic vibe.

One of the tall flutes held a special surprise. A shiny, *expensive* surprise. Sure, I knew she didn't drink, but she'd make an exception tonight. She would have to so she could receive her once in a lifetime gift.

Sweat trickled down my back and forehead. I took the linen napkin and dabbed at the little drops of moisture before they stung my eyes. For the first time in my life I was nervous, which made me chuckle. A person such as myself did not get nervous ...

should never *become* nervous.

All through the trial, with the cameras going and eyes on me, I had kept my cool, seeming calm and together. An attorney couldn't afford to show any sign of weakness. Strength and charm were needed in every word spoken, along with wisdom and aggression.

No, speaking to a large amount of people never caused butterflies in my stomach. I'd go as far as to say that I could speak to the entire world and not lose my dignified personality. But when it came to Serena...

There was something about her that made me quiver in my snake-skin shoes. Her flawless beauty, honorable disposition, soft touch, and flower-scented perfume was almost too much for me to handle. Everything about this woman made me weak in the knees. She was almost the ideal woman.

Almost.

Serena's obsession with God and going to church every time the doors opened blemished her otherwise perfectness. I held on to the hope that she would eventually outgrow these preposterous beliefs and wake up. One day she'd be too busy to attend church, especially when I swept her off to California. That's where the big bucks were made. With me, she'd never have to work another day in her life. What woman would not jump at that chance?

The door to the little restaurant opened, hitting the bell that hovered from the ceiling. Even from the back of the building I could see her radiant resplendence. As she walked toward me, my heart skipped a beat. Seriously, this woman had such a strong hold on me! She'd dressed up, too, like I'd told her in the voicemail. A black dress with spaghetti straps, the hem resting just slightly above her knees, showing off her fit legs. Her hair was styled in a twist, elongating her delicate neck. The only possession that didn't go with her outfit was the cheap, over-sized red pocketbook she carried everywhere she went. Still, she was an angel in my eyes.

Once she reached the table, I swiftly sprung up and pulled a seat out for her.

"Here, let me," I offered, using the most charming tone I could muster. As she sat I scooted her closer to the table.

"Thank you," she said softly, her eyes lowered.

"You are very welcome," I replied.

Taking my seat, I stared at her, entrapped by her captivating presence. Happiness blossomed in my chest, like a flower opening to sun rays. Images of the two of us getting married and traveling the world together snapped vividly across my mind. I imagined us going to state dinners and charity balls, speaking to influential people, the whole time her arm hanging on to me for dear life. Yes, she would be the perfect eye candy for my upcoming world. The perfect trophy wife.

"Jeff, are you okay?" she inquired. Her voice pulled me from my languorous state. Coming alive once again, I shot her with my biggest smile.

"Yeah, I'm terrific," I answered. "It's just ... do you know how astonishingly gorgeous you are? I'm one lucky fellow."

In the past, those words always brought a smile to her lips and a blush on her face. Tonight, though, she remained placid, lifting a hand to place a wayward hair behind her ear. Something was looming heavy over her mind, something I had no clue on. I figured it was because we'd been apart for a couple of weeks, so I shrugged the matter off and decided to get down to the nitty-gritty.

"I have something planned for you tonight," I informed her mysteriously. "Something so big and amazing that I can't wait to get out." I narrowed my eyes at her, becoming very serious. "Something that you can't refuse. But first, I want to make a toast."

Raising my glass of champagne, I waited as she lifted her own. She gazed at me with one eyebrow raised, her lips still unsmiling. I continued, hoping that when I popped the question she would bust out of her ostensibly depressed state.

"Serena," I began, snatching hold of her eyes, "you are my everything. My world. Ever since the day you spilled coffee all over my suit, you've had my heart." I paused, inwardly congratulating myself for my glossy words, knowing I would get her where I want her. "You are my sunshine on a rainy day. You are the reason I want to continue living. I love your brazen honesty, your work ethics, your nurturing ways. I love how your baby blues soak me into an ocean of you." Wow, that last part sounded like a song! Probably was, but who cares!

"I love you, Serena Little," I announced gallantly. "I want to give you a good life. I want to give you everything this world has to offer."

Her eyes widened with every word that came out of my mouth, words that I didn't even know I had inside me. To be brutally honest, I was feeling quite proud of myself at the moment. The flute in her hands shook and I was surprised she hadn't noticed the ring resting at the bottom. I clinked her glass, then downed my champagne. I waited for her to take a sip, but she never did. Rather she sat her flute down onto the table and let out a sigh.

Immediately I inquired, "What's the matter?"

"You know I don't drink," she quickly countered. Her chin lifted in defiance.

Whoa, that was unexpected. I knew she didn't drink, but I thought for this occasion she could lower her values a tiny bit. Also, the way she was glaring had me on edge. A fiery light burned in her eyes, and I wondered what was going through her mind.

My first instinct was to become agitated and start an argument, but tonight I reigned in that emotion, replacing it with a more sensitive one. I didn't want this night ruined because of some stupid rule she had against drinking alcohol.

"Sorry about that," I told her in phony repentance. "I'll drink yours, too." I took her flute and downed her champagne, careful not to swallow the ring. I caught the ring in my mouth, shooting her an awestruck glance.

"Wow!" I exclaimed. I stood to my feet. Taking the ring out of my mouth I exclaimed, "Would you look at that! Where did this come from?" She stood as well, a look of worry drawn on her face.

"What's the matter? Are you okay?" She placed a hand on my shoulder, waiting on my answer. I smiled at her, then dropped down to one knee. She gasped in shock, taking a step back.

"Serena Little," I began confidently, "will you marry me?"

When I raised the diamond ring, her eyes glassed over with tears and her hand raised to her chest. My heart was pounding a mile a minute as I looked up at the woman I planned to marry. I watched as a tear slid down her cheek. Wow, was she one happy woman to be marrying me!

A few moments passed by, the sound of a blissful violin the only noise surrounding us. I waited, still perched on one knee, for her to accept my offer. Instead, I received the blow of a lifetime. The answer I wasn't expecting to come from the woman I loved.

"Oh, Jeff," she breathed out. Her head shook side to side. "No. I can't marry you."

Her words nearly knocked me to the ground. What did she mean *no*? She couldn't say no! She loved me. She was always there for me. We were meant to be together. How could she say no to me, Jeff Craner?

"We need to talk," she said carefully, sitting back down. "Please ... just get up and take your seat." She glanced down at the ring, cueing her to add, "And put that thing away."

Still weighed down by heavy disbelief, I slowly made my way up and into my seat, my movement almost crippled. My heart felt like a boulder in my chest, overloaded with confusion. I placed the ring in my pocket, then took in the first woman to ever tell me no.

Before anything else was said, the waiter came up and spoke, "Good evening. Are you ready to—"

"Not right now," I snapped unpleasantly, not letting my eyes leave Serena. The waiter quickly turned away, leaving me to find out the reasons behind her negative answer. We sat in an uncomfortable silence for a long while. I was speechless, and that was not becoming of a lawyer.

"Why would you say no to me?" I marveled, breaking through the painful quietude. It took everything I had inside of me to bite back the rage that burned through my veins. "I'm a good man to you. I'd do anything for you. Is it because I don't believe in your made-up God?"

"He's not made-up," she seethed, gritting her teeth. "And yes, that is mostly why."

"Mostly?" I said back.

She nodded. "Mostly."

I watched as she leaned down, reaching into her pocketbook. When she pulled out a napkin with red lipstick coloring it, I almost lost it.

As she passed it to me she said, "I found this in one of your suit pockets."

Taking it, I glanced the piece of paper over, then laid it on the table. I had to play this cool. Let her know that this wasn't what she thought it to be. True, I knew exactly who the woman was, but it had been three months before. I hadn't talked to her since.

"I don't remember her," I lied, clasping my hands and resting them on the table. "Anyway, that happened before we got together."

"There's a date on it, Jeff," she sadly pointed out. She hoisted her eyes up, capturing my gaze. "I also know she's not the only one." She kept her stone-cold glare on me as she leaned into her pocketbook once again, this time pulling out a large manilla folder. She tossed it at me, some of its contents falling out.

A huge boulder of guilt and shame fell on top of me, my whole body a shaking leaf. I picked up my credit card statements, along with some love letters sent to me from a few of the women I'd visited on the road. Anger began to boil in my blood, but I wasn't exactly mad at myself.

I was mad because I'd gotten caught.

Chapter 4

Serena

Jeff was about to fall apart, and for a good reason, too. His girlfriend, the one he just proposed to, had found out all of his dirty secrets. I knew he was upset, probably trying to come up with a way to denounce the incriminating evidence I'd produced. What I hadn't expected was what he said next.

"You went through my belongings while I was gone?" he interrogated, his face becoming beet red. "How dare you! After all I've done for you."

For a brief moment I was caught off guard, tangled in a thick web of disbelief. I quickly regained my composure, shaking away the shock, and countered with, "How dare I? Are you kidding me?" He made an attempt to interrupt, but a swift slap across his face halted his words. This was my moment, my turn to speak.

"Jeff, how can you look me in the eyes and talk down to me like that? You've been lying and cheating this whole relationship! You've disrespected me over and over and over again. Not only have you let the devil have full reign over your flesh, you've denied God and called him fabricated. Even if I hadn't found out about you cheating on me with numerous women, I was going to end it. End *us*."

Keeping my eye strictly on him, I noticed he was squirming where he sat. With everything he'd put me through – lying, cheating, and his grandiloquent attitude – I should have been feeling a little satisfaction. I wanted to feel satisfaction in seeing him fidget in his own mess, sitting in the literal hot seat. As much as I tried, the only feeling I felt for him was pity. His sins had finally caught up with him, and he was backed into a corner of his own making.

"Serena," he finally choked out, his eyes regarding me with leaden remorse. "Look, I know I've done you wrong, but the past is the past. I screwed up, and I'm sorry. I've been a dirtbag, and I've treated you unfairly. What I can do is promise you that I'll change. No more cheating, no more lying ... I'll even give your God a shot. Please, give me another chance! Can you find it in your heart to forgive me? Can I ever earn your trust again?"

Cautiously, I ingested his words, observing his doleful expression. They were almost sincere.

After being with him for a year I'd learned his ways, and right now he was putting on an act. He was trying to trick me, but all that was over. In the past I'd stupidly let him play me, accepting his empty apologies and gifts he loved to pour over me. Throughout it all, I'd held a pinch of hope in my heart, thinking that he would come to realize that God was real. My prayers had revolved around him throwing away his selfish pride and waking up to the reality that when we leave this world it wasn't the end. That it was only the beginning when we died.

Sitting in the restaurant, listening to his sweet nothings, I knew that I had done all I could humanly do. He was an immoral man who loved money, possessions, and most recently, women ... or maybe he'd been that way all along. I had to suck it up and let God intervene.

"Jeff," I started, reaching across the table and taking his hand. "I love you. I care for you, and I will continue to pray for your soul. And of course I forgive you, but as for trust ... that's gone. It's over. There's no way we can be together. My hope for you is that you find God and get on the right path. I tried to help you, but I've learned that the only one who can help you is the Lord. But you've got to allow Him in. That part is entirely up to you."

For a few silent heartbeats, I thought I was getting through to him. He lowered his gaze down to our hands, with tears pooling in his green eyes. Maybe he was breaking down the impenetrable wall that had been built years ago. My hopes were instantly shattered when he yanked his hand from mine and stood to his feet. That's the moment I knew that every single one of my words had fallen on deaf ears. He wouldn't change. Not for me, anyway.

Putting on his coat and throwing money on the table he muttered, "That will take care of the champagne." He kept his gaze on the ground, his wall still up and thicker than ever. Before he could storm out, I sprung to my feet and seized his arm. I didn't want it to end this way.

"Jeff, wait!" I exclaimed, but from the dark look he was sporting I knew he wasn't going to take anymore from me. Taking his thumb and pointer finger, he removed my hand, wearing a disgusted facial expression.

"I tried to apologize," he drilled out through clenched teeth. Rage darkened his usual bright eyes, causing me to shudder. "I even said I'd try the church thing, but you won't give me another chance."

"But, Jeff," I pushed, willing him to listen. "You've got to see it from my position. You've cheated on me over and over—"

"Yeah, I did," he admitted without remorse, nodding his head. "And you're right ... I probably would've continued seeing other woman. Also, *darling*, there's no way you could have changed me, and there's no way I would've gone to church. That's a bunch of bull." Leaning in and narrowing his eyes he spat out, "Maybe you're the problem. Maybe you are the one who needs to *wake up*."

I stared up at him, not able to contain the tears dribbling down my cheeks. He glared back at me for a few seconds, then straightened up, adjusting his tie.

"We're done here," he announced matter-of-factly, spinning on his heels and showing me his back.

"Jeff—"

"Have a nice life, Serena!" he called over his shoulder. Strolling out of the restaurant, he slammed the door so hard the little bell that hung from the ceiling broke off.

Falling into my seat, I tried shaking off the haziness that was busy attacking my nerves. His harsh, callus words had left me numb, leading me off into an incredulous state. With all that was said and done, no matter how hard this was, the break up had to happen. He'd hurt me so many times, causing my spirit to become crushed. The worst of it was that I had not helped him at all. I'd wasted a whole year, thinking he was the one. Instead, he'd taken my heart and shoved a knife through it.

For the second time that day, tears flowed down my cheeks, and again I cried out to God to put the pieces of my heart back together.

The Messenger

Serena was, in one simple word, devastated.

I was always amazed at how the human heart could break so easily. They focused all their time and energy on hollow relationships that never worked without God. The same could be said for couples who were unbelievers, since the path they chose to tread led to death and destruction.

Serena had tried to help Jeff, but little did she know he was too far down the road of the lost. God had given him many chances to change, ample time to see that He was real. Jeff and his freewill chose darkness; eventually he would fall. Like Lucifer and a third of the angels, he would miss out on the paradise that is Heaven.

Sitting across from Serena, I felt every emotion she was feeling. Defeat, sorrow, guilt – all because she thought she had failed Jeff. She thought she'd failed God. In reality, she'd learned a grave lesson, one that she'd remember the rest of her life. God, not her or any human, could bring light into a dark soul. Only through the blood of Jesus Christ could salvation be found.

Tilting forward, I spoke in a small voice, "Call Rose. Have her meet you here."

Rose, a Godly woman herself, would stay with Serena and help her through the disaster. It would only last a season. A new season awaited Serena, but she'd have to wait another six months.

I smiled as Serena called her friend, telling her all the details quickly. Rose, a friend to the end, was already on her way.

I closed my eyes, lifted my hands above me, and gave praise to God.

The Usher

In the darkest corner of the local bar, I waited for Mr. Craner to come undone. He was sitting on a bar stool, attempting to drink his troubles away. The fool. He had no idea that he was fast-forwarding his demise.

I laughed, rubbing my hands together with anticipation. He would never recover, never get the chance to rise up from his sinful nature. Too proud and too vain to admit when he was wrong. Very similar to myself. I'd fallen because of my pride and superiority, leaving me in eternal darkness. Lucifer was my lord, and for being loyal to his kingdom, I'd been given the title "The Usher" – the one who escorted new souls into Hell. I was the welcoming committee for the dark underworld, the first one they met when the angels tossed them through the gates.

Sniffing the air, I sighed with gratification. Waves upon waves of grief rolled off Mr. Craner's body, his soul permanently damaged. His torture was my fuel, my sustenance to keep me strong. Again I saw many Holy Angels amongst little groups of people, watching the humans revel in their very open drunkenness. One of them was even sitting next to Mr. Craner in hopes of breaking through the steel curtain of his emotions.

I laughed. They could keep trying to get his attention, but they were about to be disappointed, for I knew Mr. Craner. He was like many before him, who were judged by the Almighty and sentenced to an eternity in Hell. I rubbed my hands together and grinned with satisfaction.

His downfall would be my absolute delight.

Chapter Five

Jeff

The bartender filled my shot glass up for ... I don't know, either the tenth or twelfth time. I wasn't sure how many I had swigged, since I'd stopped counting at number seven. For a man, I was a lightweight when it came to alcohol. I always stayed away from hard liquor. Tonight I'd made an exception. There wasn't any other choice in the matter.

The plan was simple – find the closest bar and get bombed. I needed to numb my mind, to completely erase Serena Little from my memory. Regrettably that chore was proving futile, propelling me to keep slugging back shots. The burn of the amber liquid slithered down my throat, taking away the gritty pain that my heart was suffering, though it only lasted a few seconds. In no time Serena snaked her way back into my mind, swimming around in the misty waves of my conscience.

Man, I had really messed up. She was perfect for me, had actually cared for me! And boy, she had it all in the looks department. My dream of her being my arm candy would never come true.

It wasn't all my fault, though. Sure, I'd slept around. I wasn't perfect, but who was in this horrible world? Truth be told, it was her fault that I had wandered down a lustful road. She'd forced me, really. A man needed physical love to release tension, especially a man of my stature. If she could have let go of that promise to her "God", we'd still be together. Her inane belief in a bogus entity was what caused our relationship to spiral out of control, essentially crashing and burning into flames of inexorable heartache.

My shot glass made a *ding* sound as I dropped it onto the counter. Waving to the bartender, I motioned for him to fill it back up. He slowly walked up, pouring the golden goodness into my small liquor holder.

"I think you've had enough, don't you?" he declared, placing the bottle of Crown back on the counter behind him.

"I'll be the one to decide that," I snarled, downing the drink and slamming it on the bar. "And as long as I'm paying, you'll do what you're told. Fill it up *again*, sir."

"Dude," he shook his head. "A couple more and then I'm cutting you off. Also, you puke, you clean it up." He brought the bottle around and gave me another brimful.

I started to argue, but a lone figure caught my attention. A woman sat by herself in a booth way in the back of the bar. From first glance I could tell what kind of woman she was ... the kind you had to pay to get to know.

"Hey, man, let me buy the rest of that bottle," I called to the barkeeper. Peering behind me I added, "And give me another shot glass."

After paying for the liquor and snatching up the shot glasses, I stood to my feet. At first I thought I was going to have to sit back down. Though I was standing still, the world seemed topsy-turvy, like I'd just stepped off of a spinning carnival ride. In reality, I was more than a little drunk, and I knew my inhibitions were low, but ... I didn't want to be alone right now.

Making a quick decision, I sauntered over to the woman and introduced myself.

The Usher

If this Mr. Craner fellow harbored one single trait, it would be his unfailing predictability. Most humans could fall into this vast category, since they were weak-minded and slaves to their flesh. However, there were a select few who didn't become trapped within the world and its many temptations. The majority, nevertheless, believed it was their absolute right to divulge in very open debauchery, experiencing instant gratification.

Mr. Craner had fallen into his father's womanizing footsteps, not to mention his lack of compassion for his fellow human being. Case in point, the great Jeffrey Randall Craner was making his way over to a prostitute, holding a bottle full of poison that I considered an intellect killer.

I watched as the drunk lawyer introduced himself, sliding into the booth to sit next to the young woman. He whispered something in her ear and she laughed, the sound a high-pitched tingle in my ears.

Glancing around this certain bar I saw many humans engaging in gossip and drunken revelry. It reminded me of one of the little brothels that had existed when Sodom and Gomorrah reigned. That had been a good time, until *He* sent two angels to destroy all the work myself and fellow comrades had achieved.

Bringing my attention to the back booth, I realized that Mr. Craner and the scantily dressed woman had gotten up and were walking out the doors of the bar. Together.

Concealed in my dark shadow, I followed the couple to a filthy hotel. I watched as they got into the elevator, kissing as the door closed.

A few angels stood around, staring at me with expressions that could only be read as outrage. Mr. Craner was about to meet his maker, and these Holy Ones were still trying to steer him away from the dark path he'd been treading for years. Their attempts were ineffectual, for Mr. Craner had dug his own grave and would pay for his venomous behavior.

The wait was almost over. I could smell it in the air. His demise had already been set. And I would be there at the appointed time. In the meantime, I had to wait.

Yes, I would wait.

Jeff

Two hours later...

After puking for the third time, I flushed the hotel room's toilet, which was stained yellow from many years of use. I splashed water in my face, cupping a little in my hand to rinse out my mouth. Picking up the hand towel and wiping my face dry, I took a gander at my reflection in the mirror. Dark circles rested under my blood shot eyes, my skin shown a sickly yellow ... of course, the dim bathroom light could have been the cause of my pallidness.

Collecting my things, I closed the door to the hotel room softly, leaving the woman passed out on the bed. I couldn't remember her name.

Two hundred dollars waited on the nightstand for her when she woke up, a hundred more than she'd charged. Little did she know that our brief interaction had helped me forget about Serena. I smiled as the elevator door closed, feeling like a huge weight had been hoisted off my shoulders.

So Serena broke it off with me, declined my marriage proposal – so *what*! Who needed her? Who needed anybody? I would do fine on my own. A huge law firm was awaiting my arrival in California, so what worries could I possible have?

The elevator door opened and I stepped out. A nasty odor assaulted my sensitive nose, making my empty stomach churn. But I didn't let that hinder my good mood. I still had a buzz going as I walked out onto the sidewalk. Glancing at my watch I was shocked to see it read almost 4:00 AM.

"Time flies when you're having fun," I said aloud, chortling at my little banter.

Eyeing my beautiful black Mercedes across the street, I started making my way over, whistling as my feet moved. My king-sized bed was calling my name, but first my muscles were aching for a sit in the hot tub.

If I hadn't been thinking so deeply on how relaxing the jets were going to feel on my tensed muscles, maybe I would've seen the bus barreling down the street. Maybe if my mind hadn't been so fuzzy from alcohol, my reflexes would have saved my life.

The last image that invaded my brain was the high beams of the bus. The last sound that assailed my ears was the abrasiveness of the bus's horn.

And then...

The Usher

Yes! Yes! YES!

This was it, the moment I'd desperately longed for!

Mr. Craner's world had been torn apart, but somewhere in the back of his mind he'd come to the conclusion that he was going to be just fine. Ha! How fickle the human mind worked! Hurting a person, being hurt in return, then paying for lustful gratification and forgetting all troubles, each day becoming less human. A damaged soul in shambles, quickly turning to ash and blowing away in the perverse winds of death.

Angels of the Most High watched the scene with sadness etched on their faces. They knew where Mr. Craner was going. All the work they'd done to try and steer him toward God was now seen as a failure, though they'd tried their best. They always did.

It wasn't their faults, really. Humans had the freewill to live their lives by their own choosing; unbeknownst to Mr. Craner, he'd signed his soul over to death.

Jubilantly, I observed his broken, mangled body as it flew through the air, the life force within him already snuffed out. A surge of power snaked through my entire being as I felt his soul became permanently detached from his flesh. He was about to meet his Maker, the one he denied existed for all his life.

Then it would be my turn.

My turn to welcome Mr. Craner to his eternity.

Chapter 6

Jeff

A bright, almost searing white light burned my eyes, causing me to shield them with my hand. I tried to blink away the dots dancing in my sight, but it would take a little time for my vision to clear. It was as if two flashlights were touching each of my corneas.

Getting my bearings, my eyes eventually getting used to the unyielding light, I took in my surroundings. I was surrounded by whiteness. A mistiness, sort of like a white fog, floated in the air, making it hard to decipher where it began or ended. Shifting my gaze left, then right, I saw that this haziness went on for miles ... possibly forever.

How had I gotten here? I'd just been out in the cold night air, crossing the street to get into my car, and now I was ... I had no idea. The only conclusion that sounded reasonable was that I'd passed out from my semi-drunken state. In other words, I had to be dreaming. That was a sane realization. I seriously hoped someone would come along and drag me off the street, because if not I would surely be a goner.

Suddenly, two figures appeared next to me, one on each side. For a moment all I could do was look at their armored bodies, shields, and swords. They wore brass helmets on their heads and stony gazes in their eyes, which exhibited incandescent colors of blue and green. They weren't looking at me; They stared straight ahead, unblinking.

What had me even more enthralled was the white feathery wings they wore on their backs. I observed them, confused, as the word "angels" biked through my mind. Why would I be dreaming of angels?

Unable to stop myself I asked, "Who are you gentlemen? And where am—"

"**Silence!**" A booming male voice quickly shut me up. I stared hard at the angels. Neither one of them had spoken, leaving me to wonder who the authoritative voice belonged to. It came from every direction, hitting my eardrums full force and shaking the ground under my feet.

The angel with curly blonde hair ordered, "Kneel before

your Creator."

I lifted my chin in defiance. "Creator? There is no—omph!"

Before I could finish my argument, I was forced to my knees. Strong hands remained clamped on each of my shoulders, keeping me entrapped. Contained like a prisoner in chains.

In this place full of warmth and light, with armor-clad angels securing me in their solid clutches, for the first time in my life I felt small, out of place. *Completely* out of my element.

"Jeffrey Randall Craner."

Not knowing exactly what was expected of me, I decided to give a reply. "Yeah, that's me." I glanced around, to the left and to the right, but I couldn't find the person that harbored the deep voice. "Where am I? I know this is just a figment of my imagination, but—" I was cut off by the deep voice before I could finish my sentence.

"A great award awaited you in Heaven. Sadly, you will never receive it." I tried to interpose, but the voice continued. **"I sent many to show My love for you, but you rejected every one of them. My laws were spoken to you, but you turned a deaf ear to My word. You closed your heart so that My love could not enter, thus the Holy Spirit had no way in. Wickedness, lust,**

49

greed, and pride kept you bound in chains, bringing forth your destruction. The world held the throne of your heart. Trivial, temporary things ruled over your heart, instead of the One who gives eternal life.

"I have searched the Lambs Book of Life, but you are not found. You have chosen darkness over light; death over life. You never knew My Son, therefore you never knew Me. Now you will be led to the place where the lost can never be found."

"Turn away from Me, for you never knew Me."

What? *What*? I tried to stand, but the angels held me in place. Anger began to well up inside me, along with another emotion I wasn't used to.

Fear.

Before I could say anything, I found myself being hoisted to my feet and dragged toward a dark tunnel. Once we were inside, we started a downward trek. The ground was uneven, covered with jagged rock. I noticed that all the warmth I'd experienced in the light was gone, replaced with a frigid temperature. Wrenching my head to the side, I glanced behind me and watched as the light grew dimmer and dimmer, until nothing but blackness surrounded me. Try as I might, I couldn't get the angels to release me. I was trapped in their superhuman, steely grips.

"This isn't real, this isn't real..." I told myself, though for some reason I knew that was untrue. Something wasn't quite right, and I was sure my sanity was slipping away, because the voice that had spoken to me ... I just knew that had to be God.

But I didn't believe in God. Didn't believe in any supernatural junk. I didn't believe in Heaven or Hell. I believed that when you died, that was it. You ceased to exist, nothing more. Something inside me, somewhere deep within my mind, was screaming at me that I had been wrong.

That I was too late.

If this were only a dream, it was the realist dream I'd ever experienced. I could feel the angels hands gripping my arms, could feel the coldness all around me, could feel my feet shuffling over the ragged pathway. Like I was awake instead of asleep. When the smell of rot and scorched flesh singed my nose, I began to question my sanity. I also became afraid.

"Where are we?" I inquired of the angels. "Where are you taking me? And what is that horrible stench in the air?"

They remained silent, ignoring my questions and continuing to take me down the dark, rank-smelling path.

Suddenly a tall iron gate was before us, lit up by torches that hung on the bars. Behind it I saw a different kind of fog, similar to the one I'd seen in the bright light. But this was different. This particular fog was thick and black, a roiling cloud of constant disturbance. I glanced down at my feet and saw a substance similar to soot layering the ground. Little particles of ash rained down around us, covering me from head to toe. The angels, however, were not touched by the falling debris, as if a shield protected them.

In the dark mist I could hear people screaming out for help. I heard people shouting for God to save them. Howls of pain and torment also sounded in the distance. A cold blanket of terror wrapped around me when the iron gates slowly creaked open. Before I knew what was happening, the angels pushed me through the gates...

****

I jumped up from the seat I appeared in. Confusion settled heavily on my mind as I took in the dark room. Four walls surrounded me, no windows or doors. How had I gotten in here? One minute I was being escorted by angels, the next I was being pushed through an iron gate, and now...

Walking around the box of a room, I inspected each wall,

hoping to find a secret doorway or passage. A dent in the middle of one caught my attention and immediately I placed my hands on it, expecting it to open or move. Instead an agonizing scream crawled out of my throat. Pulling my hands away I was appalled to see my hands overlaid with blisters, which were already swelling and oozing. I glanced at the wall, then back to my injured hands. The walls must have been made of metal, leading me to believe if I'd held my hands on its surface a few seconds longer, my flesh would have melted right off. It also led me to wonder what was behind the wall making it so smoldering hot.

A bump sounded behind me, triggering me to spin around quickly. On turning around I was stunned to see that a metal table had appeared, along with another chair opposite the one I'd sprung from. Lying on top of the table was a thick folder, with my name cryptically scrawled across it.

"The life and death of Jeffrey Randall Craner," I uttered aloud in complete disbelief. I was about to open the folder and investigate when a bone-chilling male voice vibrated through the room.

"That is not for your eyes to see."

Glancing up, I jumped back a few feet, running into the wall, which I instantly recoiled from because of the intense heat. A tall figure dressed in a black robe had materialized on the other wall. I couldn't see his face. His hood was on, and only a darkened shadow could be seen where his face should have been. Intense fear slid through my limbs as I stared at the ominous figure, unsure of what to do or say.

"At least," he continued in a grave tone, "not for your eyes to see ... *yet*."

"Who are you? Where am I?" The questions tumbled from my mouth before I could stop them.

The dark figure wasted no time on responding. "The answer to your first question ... I am known as The Usher. And as for your second question, you'll be getting that answer soon enough, though deep down I'm pretty sure you have a decent guess." I stared at him with anger coiling through my system, not at all satisfied with his reply.

"Why can't I see your face?" I countered. "I don't like speaking with someone who will not show their face."

"Oh, that bothers you?" His tone was light and curious. He tilted his hooded-head to the side. "Well, maybe this will settle your anxious nerves."

With the snap of his fingers, the hooded figure

transformed before my eyes. Instead of a cryptic form, a white man stood in its place, with a wide-set grin on his face. His hair was black, slicked back, and his chin bore a short goatee. The suit he wore was similar to the one I had on – black pin-striped with a black tie. His eyes ... whoa, his eyes caused a squeamish feel in the pit of my stomach. They were black as the night sky; black as a deep, dank well. A tinge of red sat in each pupil, glowing slightly.

My mouth had fallen agape in extreme shock. I tried to speak but couldn't form the syllables needed. It was at that very moment I noticed that this room was *extremely* hot. Sweltering and miserable. Beads of perspiration dripped into my eyes, stinging me in the process.

"Is this better?" the man smirked, his eyebrows raised.

"What are you?" I cautiously inquired. "And what do you mean by *usher*?"

"Maybe you should sit down," he sighed, taking his seat while motioning to mine. "And feel free to shake out of that jacket. Loosen your tie and get as comfortable as you can, because we have a lot of ground to cover."

I snickered at his words, which reminded me of the dialog I used with clients.

"What are you, a lawyer?" I quipped, chuckling at my sarcasm.

His lips curled, replying, "I'm a lawyer of sorts, I suppose."

"Is that a fact?" I asked, shrugging out of my jacket and carefully folding it on the back of the seat. I slumped down in the chair and untied my tie, using it as a towel to wipe the sweat off my face and out of my eyes. Taking off my jacket had done little to help the heat. If anything it felt hotter than before.

"I cannot tell a lie ... or can I?" He laughed at his own banter, but I didn't find it funny. I was ready to find out what was going on, how I'd gotten here ... find out where I was. And why I'd left a place of comfort and light to this unpleasant, hot room.

"You'll find out soon, I promise," he told me, his happy features replaced with profound sincerity. "And that place of light and comfort – don't worry. You'll never see that place again." His words caught me off guard.

"What will I find out? And why won't I see that place again?" I observed his facial expression, trying to figure him out. That's what helped me with many cases in the past, watching for anything that might discredit the witness. With this guy, though, I was picking up absolutely nothing.

"You know," he said, tapping his head. "Your thoughts tell me everything I need to know about you."

I chuckled. "Oh, so you're some kind of mind reader, huh? Yeah, *right*." I waited for him to join in on my laughter, but he never did. He continued to stare at me with an unreadable look coloring his pale face.

"Actually, yes, Mr. Craner. I know everything about you. Your past, your present. I even know your future, but first we are going to talk about how you got here."

"Awesome, that's what I've been waiting for." I blew out a sigh of relief. "I don't know why I'm here, but I'd like to get this over with so I can go home and get some rest. Also, could you tell someone to turn on the air conditioning?" I wiped my face again with my tie, which was already sopping wet.

"Oh, Mr. Craner," he said, adding a *tsk tsk* and shaking his head. "There is no air conditioning here, so you'll have to learn how to deal. And as for going home – you are home."

Shooting him a quizzical look, I quickly countered, "Uh, no, this is not..." A sudden thought popped in my mind, bringing my sentence to a halt. It was finally starting to make sense.

"Wait a minute ... wait just one minute!" I chortled loudly, slapping the top of my thigh. "This is a prank, it has to be! Gerald's name is written all over it." Leaning my elbows on the table, it was starting to make sense.

Gerald, one of my closest friends, and I had been playing pranks on each other since our college years. This was all an elaborate prank to make me think I was dead. Yeah, this was a pretty decent joke. It would take me years to top this one.

"This isn't a prank," informed the mysterious man, matching my movements by inclining his own elbows a top the table. "Besides, Gerald *hates* you." His harsh proclamation left me dismayed.

"Gerald doesn't hate me," I indicated severely, becoming irritated with this stranger. "He's been my friend for years!"

He shook his head adamantly. "Nope. He despises you. And being a lawyer I'm surprised you didn't catch on to how much he can't stand you."

"No," I vehemently spoke, my skepticism growing. "You are wrong."

He leaned over, just inches from my face. "He thinks you're a pompous jerk who doesn't deserve the life you have ... well, the life you had."

"What do you mean *had*?"

Sighing and leaning back against his chair, he asked, "What's the last thing you remember before arriving here?"

I busily thought back to my day. It had gone well at first – winning the case of a lifetime, learning I'd been offered a great job, and preparing to ask Serena to marry me. That's when everything started rolling downhill. Serena dumped me and I'd walked a few buildings down to my favorite bar in attempts to mend my broken heart. A beautiful lady walked in, we got a hotel room, and...

Afterward I'd gone outside and found my car parked across the street. I stepped onto the street, walking toward my car, when a bus was coming at me...

Then I appeared in a bright place where armored angels held onto me while I listened to an unseen voice. Afterward they dragged me through a dark tunnel that ended with me being pushed through a gate and suddenly in the room I was in presently.

A hard rock of realization pounded inside of me, causing my insides to lurch with an overwhelming panic.

"Oh no," I uttered aloud, gazing down at myself and patting my chest. My shirt was soaked through with sweat. How was it possible for this room to be getting hotter."

"What is it, Mr. Craner?"

Shifting my gaze up to stare into the man's unusual eyes I whispered, "It can't be. I ... It can't be."

"Can't be what?" The man's unblinking orbs glared me down, hooking me into their darkening depths.

"That bus hit me. I'm dead."

Chapter 7

The Usher

A selfish, giddy sensation coursed through my tainted blood at what was about to take place. Sentencing this evil man to an eternity in Hell would be extremely delicious. This was my favorite part, even more that watching humans ruining their souls daily by rejecting the man upstairs. Yes, this certain part was the most rewarding. It let my boss know how great a job I was doing in adding souls to his demented kingdom.

Mr. Craner sat across from me, at last figuring out that he didn't exist in the land of the living any longer. He finally knew the truth, that there was definitely life after death. Fear and madness seeped out from every pore in his body, and I inhaled deeply, the emotions filling my being with scrumptious pleasure. An evil grin spread across my face.

"Yes, Mr. Craner, you are dead, but your soul still thrives."

I paused, gauging his reaction to my words. I could hear his uneasy, muddled thoughts, which sounded glorious to my ears. I continued my speech, all the while keeping my malicious smirk. "Before you try a rebuttal, I'm going to explain your reality. Despite what you thought when you were alive, there is life after death. There is a Heaven," I spat the disgusting word out, "and there is a Hell ... which is where you find yourself today."

"No," he expressed deplorably, his eyes glassing over with tears. "No, this isn't ... this isn't right."

"Oh, but it is," I replied gleefully, eager to start the next phase. For me to do this, I opened the folder which held Mr. Craner's entire life inside. Opening it up, I glanced over the pages. "My, my, my, what a privileged life you lived! You grew up in a mansion, surrounded by maids and nannies. Hmm, seems you had a little affair with one of your babysitters when you were fourteen. That appears to be the age you became a deviant little fiend, am I right, Mr. Craner?"

"I-I don't know..." he stammered, his body shaking like a thin piece of paper. Sweat was now dripping down his arms and neck, his body just in the beginning stages of Hell's climate.

"Your mother and father gave you everything you asked for and more," I proceeded on, going through his life record. "Of course they thought you were a little angel, didn't they? They didn't know about the money you stole from the safe, or the many teenage girls you brought into their bed while they were on luxurious vacations. They didn't know about the parties with alcohol and drugs you had in their mansion, or the rape that occurred at one of them ... of course, they weren't the perfect role models for a teenage boy, or anyone for that matter. They're full of the devil themselves. I'm sure one day I'll get to meet them both."

"Now, pressing forward to more of your diabolical actions," I declared, flipping to the middle of his folder. Lifting my gaze, I raised an eyebrow at him. "It seems your college days were full of sin and shame as well. Cheating on tests, selling out your own friends for grades, numerous sexual adventures with many partners. Wow, did you know one of your trysts ended up in an unwanted pregnancy? Oh, of course you do! You paid for the abortion yourself."

He gawked at me, stunned at my knowledge. "How do you know – "

"I know," I interjected swiftly, "because it is my job. I've been watching you for a long time, Mr. Craner. I know your thoughts, actions, lies. Greed and power were your goals on earth. That brings us to your most recent foul-ups."

Turning a few more pages, I lifted a picture of Billy Fitz, the child molester and all around malevolent human being. "The day you died you had won the case that would've sent you to a higher status on earth. You helped get a child molester free ... oh, and will you look at this! He's already on the prowl, hunting for his next victim. And this time he's preying on a little six year old boy. Bravo, Mr. Craner! Bravo! What an outstanding citizen you were!"

"You can't possibly know that," he remarked, though his tone was defeated.

"I've got the picture to prove it." I showed him a picture of Billy Fitz, who was watching a little boy playing alone in the park.

"No," he murmured, taking in the picture in shock.

"Oh yes," I grumbled, tossing the picture aside. "You didn't know it, but you were working for Satan the whole time."

He covered his face with his hands, moaning, "This can't be happening."

Another round of excitement touched my black heart as I soaked in his raw, tortured emotions. Turning to the last page, a smile crept across my lips at what I saw. This would be his breaking point, bringing him to the point of wishing he could have it all back; wanting a second chance, so he could go back and do more for humanity. More importantly, take the only woman he'd ever loved more seriously, and believe in something other than himself.

Jeff Craner knew the truth now, but it was too little too late.

"Serena Little." The two words came out of my mouth in a mocking fashion. I watched with interest as his face turned red, his pulse beginning to beat with red-hot rage.

"Don't you dare bring her into this!" he bellowed, his voice radiating throughout the room.

I cackled. "What is it, Mr. Craner? Did I strike a nerve? Is this a touchy subject for you?"

"Sort of, yes. She is ... was important to me."

I gave a solid nod. "Ah, so that's why you cheated on her with various women. You also thought yourself a little above her, didn't you? After all, you were a prestigious lawyer with nice suits and a load of cash, while she's a lowly Kindergarten teacher that has enough faith to move mountains. Bet you're wishing you'd listened to that woman."

I waited for him to fire off a retort, but it didn't come. The veins in his neck were popping out, and a breeze of sorrow was wafting off of him in short bursts.

"My, my, my," I jeered, whistling at a picture of Serena Little. "What a lovely specimen. Though you messed that up, too. Didn't you? Just like everything in your past."

He held out his hand and ordered, "Let me see that."

"She will mourn you," I said, keeping his buttons pushed. "Though only for a season. From what I gather she'll meet someone in a few months and get married. Eventually she'll forget all about you. Just like your parents have."

"Give me that!" he snarled angrily, snatching the picture from my hand and flying to his feet. A look of sadness touched his expression as he brushed his fingertips across it. When the picture caught fire and turned to ashes, he stood there in total perplexity. I laughed again – this was getting good!

"It seems, Mr. Craner, that you ruin everything you touch."

"What just..." He trailed off when he noticed his hands. I knew what he was thinking, but decided to let him have a go at this one.

"What is it now?" I breathed out, feigning boredom. He sat

back down in his seat, still staring down at his palms.

"My hands," he began, his voice shaky with doubt. "When I touched the walls earlier, they were burned and had blisters, and now—"

"They are blemish free," I finished for him.

"Yeah, but that's impossible."

"Let me see them," I commanded firmly. He did what he was told. I liked that he was quickly becoming obedient. I seized his hand tightly and issued a deep, long scratch on his palm. Crimson blood spilled from the wound.

"What, are you crazy or something?!" he shouted, attempting to free his hand from my grasp. It was a futile mission. He could never be as strong as I.

"Watch this, Mr. Craner," I patiently instructed, watching his face with amusement. Horror passed over his face as the wound began stitching itself back together. A few seconds later his hand was good as new. I let him go and leaned back in my seat, placing my hands on the desk.

"That's impossible," he pondered, his stricken expression almost comical.

When he shifted his gaze back to me I explained, "It's possible here. You see, Hell is a place for torture, despair, pain, and iniquity. Doomed souls are sentenced here for all eternity, each one experiencing their own unique punishment. Your hand regenerating is just a little taste of what you get here. Why, I could cut out your heart and burn it up with my bare hands. The pain would be tremendous, but the worst part is when your heart grows back. I hear the growing back part is more agonizing than the cutting out part.

"There are some going through that as we speak, only it could be arms, legs, even heads being cut off, then regeneration takes place so it can happen all over again. A never-ending cycle of torture, pain, and suffering that lasts all eternity long."

Mr. Craner's thoughts were stirring up many different emotions and feelings, each one fueling my desire to go ahead and sentence him, but I was waiting on that one certain mentation that would truly defeat him. I didn't have to wait long, for his next words shut this case forever, his life reaching its full completion.

"This is real," he said softly, staring off into space. "I'm dead and I'm in Hell."

Finally he came to the actualization that this wasn't a prank. Now I could finish this and send him on his way. Pity, really. I was beginning to have some fun.

But ... duty calls!

Standing to my feet, I shrugged off the disguise I'd been using, transforming into my normal attire. Wearing my black robe I stood almost seven feet tall, only this time I allowed Mr. Craner to see my face. When he looked up and took in my appearance, he expelled a high-pitched scream. He flew out of his chair and banged against the wall, which burned him on impact, the pain excruciating to his sensitive skin. He fell to his knees in total anguish, both physical and mental. A laugh bubbled out of me, humored by the way he'd reacted to my true physical body. My deep red skin and long horns protruding from my forehead always made humans go ballistic with sheer terror.

Oh, how I loved my job!

"Stand to your feet, Jeffrey Randall Craner!" I bellowed, declaring, "It is now time to face your eternity!"

On shaky legs, he stood, and I was pleased to see he was crying. He peeked up at me with thick tears in his eyes.

"Please, please, give me another chance!" he pleaded, speaking through wrenching sobs. "I can make this right! I can go back and live right! Please, not this! Not like this!"

"On earth, you were a man of power, money, and stature. Here, you are only a speck of nothingness, a smudge of nonexistence." I meandered over and bent down, becoming nose to nose with him. "You lived in the world, letting your sinful nature take over. Your flesh lusted after women, greed controlled your heart, and you let your conscience dwindle away to nothing. You had no compassion for your fellow man, you cheated people you called friends, you hurt the ones that loved you the most by divulging in lustful pleasures.

"As a lawyer you helped along many criminals who were blatantly guilty, but you didn't care. You worked hours and hours to free a man who hungered for small children to take and ruin. You sold your soul to worldly possessions, money, mansions, and for what?" I gave him a chance to answer, but he never did. He was too busy blubbering like an infant and begging for mercy.

"I'll answer for you," I revealed, taking two steps away. "You sold your soul so you could spend an eternity of suffering." I flicked my wrist upward and the wall standing behind Mr. Craner blew away. Tornado like winds infiltrated the room, forcing him to grab onto the table so he wouldn't be torn away. An orange glow lit the proximity of the room, and the heat spiked to boiling. None of this had an affect on me. I was used to the climate here in Hell.

"What's happening? Oh, what's happening?!" He was hysterical, fear overtaking the sadness he'd been overwhelmed with. When he saw the fire that awaited him, screams of horror ripped from his mouth, his knuckles turning white from grasping the table so tightly. His legs were in the air, the soles of his expensive shoes beginning to melt from the overbearing heat.

Snarling I explained, "You denied your Maker and have been sentenced to an eternity in Hell, Mr. Craner. And look ... some more escorts have arrived."

Strolling through the fire were the most vicious, ugly beasts that had ever been created. Mr. Craner peered over his shoulder and I laughed out loud at his facial expression, which was full of sheer panic. The sight of these demons caused him to hold on even tighter to the table. I smiled as four of my brethren entered the room, all huge and disfigured. They would have been called monstrosities in the earthly realm. In Hell, I called them family.

"Brothers, welcome," I told my comrades, my tone brimming over with giddiness – my lord would be so excited that we'd won another soul for the dark kingdom. "This is Mr. Craner. Please take him to the place he'll spend the next, well ... forever!" I laughed, and so did my brothers. They easily lifted him and began carrying him into the fire, when I shouted, "Wait!"

They turned around and glared at me, annoyed that I'd halted their steps. Mr. Craner looked at me with a tinge of hope gleaming out of his eyes.

"Please," he continued to beg. "I don't want to go in there."

"Well, you should have thought of that when you were alive," I pointed out. Picking up the folder that contained his whole life I announced, "The man that once was is now forgotten." His folder burst into flames in my hand, leaving ashes to float to the ground.

"Have a nice eternity, Mr. Craner," I quipped, throwing my head back and laughing. I motioned for my comrades to press forward, and as they did Mr. Craner's harrowing squeals filled my ears with pleasure.

Epilogue

Jeffrey Randall Craner

Serving an eternity in Hell...

It's strange. I'm dead, but I can still feel pain. It's excruciating, enough so that most people would black out. I'm not allowed such mercy. No matter how much I want to fade away, I can't. They won't let me. The monsters who deal out my punishments are ruthless. They belittle me every second of my existence in this sinister place. Every fiber of my being suffers a constant torrent of horrendous agony.

Unstoppable. Continuous. Hurt.

The Usher had been right. Didn't matter what limb they tore off of me, whether it be an arm or an eyeball, it always grows back. Everything grows back.

I am chained to a rock wall, the jagged edges piercing into my back. My clothes are gone, leaving me stark naked and utterly exposed to whatever torture they have planned for me next.

There's always torment here. The demons never take breaks. I can hear others around me, their screams echoing throughout the land of Hell. Just like me, they're being punished, suffering through their own personal damnation. And as for the smell ... well, it's atrocious. There's nothing I can compare it to.

The climate here is unbearable. Sometimes hot lava flows down the sides of the rock I'm chained to, pouring on top of me and melting the skin off my bones. My flesh quickly grows back, just to melt off again and again. That's just one of many punishments I am made to go through. No breaks. No rest. Only continual agonizing discomfort. All the *time*.

Forever.

I think of Serena a lot. Her smile, her warmth, her goodness ... I miss her dearly. Part of my sentence is watching Serena on earth. It is hard, because I see her fall in love and get married. She has two kids, a boy and a girl. If I'd been a believer, if I'd been a different man, that could have been me by her side. But the reality is, I'm not. On earth I had been a wicked man, and I'd treated Serena with disrespect. Now she has someone who genuinely loves her. A Godly man. She deserves a happy life.

The monsters make me watch my old client, Billy Fitz, the child molester I'd proved innocent, when in actuality he'd been guilty. They make me observe his grotesque display of stalking young boys and girls, picking them up, and doing terrible, monstrous, unthinkable things to them. I try to close my eyes, not wanting to witness what is happening to these children, knowing that it's my fault they are being damaged, but the monsters take care of that by cutting my eyelids off. Sure, they regenerate, but if I close them again, they'll just cut them off. And they grow back. Over. And over. Again.

Through all the pain, all the dreadful punishments I'm forced to surrender to, they show me little peeks of what could have been. If I'd been a believer and died, I'd have gone to Heaven. I can see brief glimpses of what it's like, a peace like no other can be found there. Though I cannot watch long, because the light from there is so bright it singes my corneas, blinding me until they mend.

This is it.

This is my existence.

I will never have a chance for redemption.

My fate has already been sealed.

Hell is my eternity.

ETERNITY

- Story 2-

Jenna Kay Pridgen

Sin is no longer your master, for you no longer live under the requirements of the law. Instead, you live under the freedom of God's grace.

Romans 6:14

******

But thank God! He gives us victory over sin and death through our Lord Jesus Christ.

1Corinthians 15:57

Prologue

The Usher

Howls of anguish and despair sound throughout the bowels of Hell. I gazed out the window of my office, enjoying the view, basking in the scorching climate which held many human souls in its unabated diabolical captivity. Each soul was experiencing different degrees of intense torment in this desolate underworld. Many, many more souls were on their way to begin their eternal damnation. I smiled at that particular thought. Death made me happy; Torture made me deliriously giddy.

Any other demon would be overwhelmed with the huge pile of files inhabiting the desk, all chock-full of broken, defeated souls waiting to be welcomed to Hell. I, however, was not the least bit upset with my busy schedule. That was why my boss had gifted me this job. Though being able to send out lower ranking demons helped to make my workload not so arduous.

Really, the job wasn't too difficult. Wicked humans walking the earth did the majority of the work, since most were filled thick with unrelenting sin. The "whatever makes you feel good" mentality helped secure many a soul in harrowing fiery prisons, their actions defining their agony.

Sniffing the air, I allowed an over-sized sneer to take hold of my black, cracked lips. My subordinate, Pharmakeia, had finally arrived to give his latest report on his assignment, Justine Stancil.

"Well, Pharmakeia, so glad you decided to show." I spun around and narrowed my eyes, taking the seat behind my desk. "And only five hours late."

Pharmakeia made no move to sit. He knew his ruptured sores and boils disgusted me, along with his putrid, decaying smell. He could not help the way he'd been created. Toxins and disease riddled his entire existence, filling every pore and crevice on his disastrous body. Standing at ten feet tall, his extra long arms rested at his sides, his fingertips nearly touching the ground. A baffling, unimaginable sight.

Pharmakeia's job was to push humans, who were clueless

of his presence, to ruin their bodies, encouraging them to indulge in mind-altering drugs and alcohol. The whole reasoning behind his creation was to make sure drug-addicted mortals continued to fill their veins with stinging poison that would eventually kill them, landing them in the lake of fire. Statistics proved that Pharmakeia excelled in his work, and Justine had been trapped in his clutches for the last twelve years.

Yes. Excelled in every drug-induced field, indeed.

"I am sorry for my tardiness, master. More and more humans are falling victim to their addictive behaviors. I am a very busy spirit."

I cringed the whole time he spoke. His voice sounded like he'd gargled with broken glass. The only way to describe his voice was to scrape metal against metal and someone choking on their own blood. Terrible and great at the same time.

"That's wonderful news, Pharmakeia," I congratulated as warmly as a demon such as I could. "At this time, however, you are ordered to stay by Justine Stancil, and her only."

He angled his head, the little movement causing a number of blisters on his neck to explode. I bit back my sudden revulsion. "Why is that, master? She is well under my authority. She is never sober, and when she sees sobriety around the corner, she quickly sells her flesh for her next hit."

"Yes, yes, that's all well and good," I quickly replicated. "But, there has been talk that a sort of intervention is in her near future."

"An intervention?" he pronounced slowly, cocking a blistered eyebrow. I sighed, reminding myself that he wasn't the brightest bulb in Hell's light bulb stack.

"The Light is planning an interference using Justine's sister," I explained.

"So why can't you send a few lesser demons to scare her off?"

"The sister is protected by the *Holy Spirit*," I spat out, the name burning the tip of my tongue.

If it were possible for Pharmakeia to pale, this would have been the moment. Since the fall, us demons were unable to say the Almighty's name – any of them, in any language. When we had let go of that disgusting paradise, made up of incandescent light and rebelled against *Him*, the utterance of His name made us physically ill.

Gulping down a ball of dread he inquired, "What are your orders, master?"

"Up your attacks," I answered with stern finality, standing to my feet and turning away from his nauseating sight. "As soon as she drops from one high, quickly make a new high available. When she encounters those from The Light, manipulate her mind by whispering words of negativity and delirium in her ears. Squash and destroy any good deed when she's approached with hope. Twist words of encouragement into discouragement full of dead optimism. It is imperative that you keep this Justine preoccupied with escaping reality. We have worked nonstop for many years on securing this soul, and you, my dear Pharmakeia, must make sure her soul stays on Hell's roll sheet. Do you understand?"

A moment passed by before he replied, "Yes, master. Will there be anything else?"

I peered over my shoulder and simply responded, "Do not fail."

Shifting my gaze back to the window, I stared down at the torrid nirvana before me. I could see human souls going through horrors unthinkable to mortals on earth. Body parts flying in the air, skin being peeled off bone, blood flowing down the pathways like crimson rivers.

A wondrous sight, indeed. I reveled in the barbarous

chorus of uninterrupted infliction. My dark bedtime melody.

I knew the exact moment Pharmakeia left, because his stench of rotted insides followed behind him. Usually I'm not anxious about an intervention from The Light on a soul so close to eternal damnation, but this Justine woman had me feeling wary. Something wasn't settling well in my dark heart, a type of raw and inexplicable cognition poking at my diminutive conscience. A wave of dread poured over me as I recognized what was happening. The Light wanted Justine, but we wanted her more.

Yes.

We wanted her more.

Chapter 1

Justine

"Come on, girl," my stepfather growled. He dragged me down the darkened hall, nearly pulling my arm out of its socket. Kicking the door open to his "special" room, he threw me inside. He stripped me naked and placed me on a large wooden table, where he proceeded to tie my hands above my head with electrical wire. Then he bound my feet to the table, leaving me completely vulnerable and exposed.

"So pure, so precious," he whispered, his eyes groping every inch of my young body as he unbuckled his pants.

Trying to fight was useless. I was powerless against him, being only fourteen years old and unnaturally malnourished. One time I had tried to fight back. I'd threatened to tell my mother what he was doing to me almost every night, but in return he'd threatened to kill both my mom and little sister. For that reason I stayed quiet, allowing him to do *whatever perverse thing he desired to my body. I never understood why he craved to take away my innocence again and again. I was just a girl.*

This had been happening since I was twelve. After two years of these nightly routines, I thought this was normal. But somewhere in the deep recesses of my mind I knew this was wrong. I didn't deserve this, though I had no choice. I had to protect my mother; I had to protect Jenny.

As his body hovered over mine, I pinched my eyes closed. Like many nights before, I tried to find a happy place while he did what he did to me.

Unfortunately, I never found such a place.

I felt everything.

****

I awoke quickly from the dream, which was more of a memory, and cringed when a pounding headache hit me. It felt like someone was throwing a sledgehammer against my skull, over and over ... and over again. Nausea assaulted my stomach, and for a moment I thought I would vomit. Luckily it slowly ebbed away. I leaned my head against the wall. That's when I realized I wasn't on the streets.

Somehow I'd managed to wind up in a worn-down diner,

one I frequently visited to get out of the cold. I didn't know how I'd ended up here. Most likely the man who'd paid for my services brought me here, which didn't happen often. Usually after an appointment, and after I'd taken whatever drug they handed me, I was thrown out in the streets like trash. Sometimes they were nice enough to put me in a box on the side of the street, but that didn't occur often.

A groan escaped my mouth. My headache continued to grow in intensity. I knew to expect this. The glorious euphoria that filled my veins when I first soaked in the chemicals – truly an amazing feeling. The sad part? The feeling didn't last. It never lasted. Eventually the drug wore off, and a pain near unbearable replaced the short moment of pure bliss. Physical pain. Emotional pain.

The fall was the worst of all. That's when my memories came back to haunt me.

Whenever I lost full control of my conscience, thoughts of my past violated my mind with all too real images. My father left when I was five years of age. Jenny, my baby sister, had just turned one. With my father out of the picture that had left my mom in a deep depression. That is, until she met Ricky, who later became my stepfather.

After he moved in, he instantly began abusing me sexually, scarring me for life. At the age of fourteen I'd been kicked out, taking to the streets. That's where I met a guy named Pete, and he introduced me to the only way to erase my past – Meth.

Of course there was no way to permanently delete my childhood. That's why I was always searching for more. I never had money, though most of the dealers used or "pimped-out" my body as payment.

Over the years I'd tried every kind of hypnotic drug there was. I've sniffed, injected, and swallowed anything and everything I could earn on the streets. Didn't matter what the drug was, I'd take it. Didn't matter at all. As long as I got to escape from my present reality, and my wounded past, I didn't care whether I swallowed a pill or pushed a needle in my vein. Release – no, *freedom* was all I wanted to achieve in this pitiful life, though in between the release and fall was utter hell.

"Justine."

Someone said my name. A face popped into my line of vision, but it was extremely blurred. I blinked a few times, shaking my head in hopes of lifting the cloudy veil from my eyes. Finally, after a few short seconds, the face became clear. The diner's owner. The old man's name was Don. I think.

"Don? Is that ... is..." I tried to form words, but my tongue felt quadruple the size it should have been, most likely swollen from the toxins in my body. My mouth felt as dry as the Arizona desert.

He placed a steamy cup of coffee in front of me. "Come on, drink this."

"Thank you," I mumbled, taking a small sip. The hot liquid burned my belly, causing my stomach to lurch. I pushed the Styrofoam cup to the side, fighting the urge to vomit. Don released a sigh.

"Do you have a place to stay tonight?" he probed, his kind eyes observing me with sadness.

"Yes," I answered outright, which was a total lie. Don knew that, too. He knew I was homeless, but there wasn't anything he or anyone could do to save me. I chose to live on the streets. It was all I knew. My choice, my rules, my life.

"Okay, then," Don muttered, knowing there was nothing else he could do. Sliding something wrapped in foil across the table he added, "Here's a BLT for the road. That should keep your hunger at bay ... until tomorrow." His tone was sad, and when he turned around I saw his shoulders slump over.

Don had been helping me for the last five years. He made sure I had at least one meal a day, supplying food, water, and coffee. He was like a grandfather to me. The only thing he couldn't do was save me from my destructive self. He couldn't take away the nightmarish memories that haunted me every waking moment of my worthless life.

Walking out the doors of the diner, eating my delicious sandwich, I bumped into one of my homeless friends. I think her name was Candy – or maybe it was Carrie? Carol? I really didn't know. Names I could never remember. Faces were easier for me to process.

"Hey, Justine," her raspy voice greeted. She stood a few inches shorter than me and wore her mousy brown hair right in her face.

"Hey," I replied with a mouth full of food, heading toward my favorite alley. She fell in step with me. I allowed it. Maybe she had a blanket or two to share. Also, a box or tent. Smelled like rain was on the way.

"Whatcha eatin'?" she asked, her eyes on my sandwich. She was as bony as I, probably fighting starvation.

"BLT," I answered, deciding to give her half. "Here ya go."

Her eyes grew wide and she smiled, showing off her yellow teeth. "Thanks, hon! As always, you take care of me. Don't ya, Justine?" She bit off half the sandwich, chewing and moaning at the same time. "Oh man, this is *good*!"

I smiled. I knew half a sandwich wouldn't fill me up, but I couldn't let her starve. "Don't mention it. Hey, you have a place we can stay? I think it's going to rain."

"Sure," she answered, scarfing down the rest of the sandwich. "And since ya shared your dinner, I'll share my *dessert*."

"Dessert?" I wondered.

"Oh yeah." She reached into her coat pocket and pulled out two syringes.

A smile brushed my dried lips as I took one for myself...

****

The rain assailed my skin like small, sharp rocks. Lifting my head I observed the numerous raindrops falling from the gray sky. They were colored orange, thanks to the lamppost my back leaned against. My friend, Carrie or Candy – whatever – was perched next to me, her unblinking eyes staring upward.

"Hey," I muttered, softly elbowing her side, "we never found a tent or … or..."

My words trailed off. I watched as Candy – Carrie – my *friend* slowly fell over, her head hitting the concrete with a *thud*. Her eyes remained wide open and vacant. Rain water pooled in her opened orbs, and I was wondrously amazed that she wasn't blinking.

"Doesn't that bother you?" I inquired, but she didn't answer; didn't look at me. She must be one of those people that slept with their eyes open. A little creepy, if you ask me.

Turning my attention back to the mesmerizing rain, I reached my hand out and watched in childlike curiosity as each drop landed in my palm. I could almost count every drop, for they were falling in slow motion.

In this brief simple moment I felt like everything was okay. Amazing. I felt amazing. I felt so amazing I forgot about my friend laying wide-eyed on the ground, the rain buffeting her unconscious body. I felt like the memories of my past were long gone, that they could never torment me again. I felt so amazing that I didn't notice that someone had sat on their knees in front of me. Not until they spoke up.

"Hey, is this her?"

A man. Asking someone a question. I'd heard him loud and clear, but didn't acknowledge his presence. Too entranced by the raindrops pooling in my hand. How had I ended up here? Didn't matter. I was feeling too good for anything to matter.

Another figure approached, then spoke. A female voice this time. With her appearance, the rain seemed to stop, which left me discomfited. A round, clear sphere hovered over me, guarding me from the rain. An umbrella, maybe? Yes, I believed so.

"Yeah," the woman confirmed, sounding out of breath. "That's her. Justine."

She knew my name. This woman knew my name. How? Who was she? I didn't know her name, but she knew...

Losing control of myself, I closed my eyes, falling back into the dark recesses of my mind.

Chapter 2

Jenny

I'd done it. I had finally found her. My big sister, Justine. Though she wasn't big, not at all. Appearing overwhelmingly skinny, her shoulder blades peeked through her soaked shirt. I was pretty sure she was malnourished and lacking accurate nutrition. Her dark blonde hair could have been mistaken for a tangled tumbleweed, and her complexion was ruddy and bruised.

Justine looked different from what I remembered. I'd been ten the last time I'd seen her, and she fourteen, so of course she didn't look the same. I knew I didn't.

We were both women now, grown up, though I had to outweigh my big sister by at least forty pounds. Her cheeks were sunk in, and heaviness sat underneath each of her eyes. By her weedy appearance, she seemed older than her twenty-six years.

When we'd approached the two homeless women, I was shocked to see that she was one of them. Nearly five years of searching had passed, and honestly, I thought the day would never come when my sister and I would reunite. I'd almost lost hope.

Almost.

The statistics on finding loved ones lost to the streets were extremely low. With that knowledge I'd been left assuming she was deceased, lost to me forever.

Today God had answered my prayer, one that I'd been speaking for years.

My friend, Chase, busied himself by checking the woman laying on the ground. Taking in her glassy eyes, I could see that the light had already parted from them.

"Is she?" I asked quietly, though I already knew the answer. I watched as he checked her pulse.

"She's gone." He took off his jacket and covered the woman's face, showing respect. He frowned up at me. "Another one lost to the streets."

Before I could respond, Justine's body began shaking uncontrollably, which immediately turned on my action switch.

"Call an ambulance, quick! She's seizing!"

"I'm on it!" Chase pulled out his cell phone and dialed.

Tossing the umbrella away, I placed my own jacket around Justine's shoulders. Pulling her into my lap, I rocked her back and forth, attempting to sooth her. I wasn't sure if it helped, but I had to try. Her hair was matted to her head. Gazing down I could see little nits hanging on her hair follicles. She had lice, but I didn't care. She stunk of body odor and mildew, but I didn't care. The rain came down faster, soaking me to the bone, but I hardly felt it. I'd just found my sister after years of searching, and she needed help.

I wasn't letting her go for anything.

****

Justine

"Better not tell your mother, girl," Ricky *warned, his hand caressing my face. "If ya do, your ma and sister are dead. You hear me. Dead." With that last word, he roughly slapped my face and walked out. A soft "click" sounded as the door closed. I was alone – alone to suffer in misery.*

I scooted off the table, standing on wobbly legs. My wrists and feet were bruised, my lips swollen from his harsh, unloving kisses. My whole body ached and my stomach felt sick, twisted into a ball of queasy sorrow.

Picking my clothes off the floor, I opened the door and tiptoed down the hall to the bathroom. I didn't want to wake my mother. I stepped into the shower and turned it to scalding hot. With my body emerged under the shower head, I scrubbed and scrubbed at my skin, wanting the smell of him and what he'd done off of me, while I cried silent tears into the steamy water. No matter how hard I washed, no matter how much soap I used, he was still there, tormenting me. I could wash my skin, but my scars ran deeper than that.

This was very routine for me, how almost every night went. Ricky arriving home late, drunk, snatching me out of bed, and raping me. Mom had no idea, and she never could. He was a stern, serious man. He never issued empty threats. I was his slave, his plaything. I was utterly trapped, and unremittingly broken. Over and over again.

When the hot water turned to ice cold, I turned off the shower and stepped out. I grabbed an already used towel from the floor and tried my best to dry off. Wrapping my long hair in the towel, I began to put my clothes on. I froze when I caught sight of my reflection in the mirror. Who was this girl staring back at me? She looked way older than her fourteen years, with her pallid skin and dark circles under her eyes. Her *usually bright blue eyes were dull and full of despair.*

"What happened to you?" I asked my reflection. My eyes saw something moving behind me, something tall and loathsome.

Long, stretchy arms reached out for me, and before I could scream its clawed hands wrapped around my mouth and pulled me backward....

I jerked awake, screaming for help. Somehow I'd made it into a bed, one that was inclined. My heart was pounding a mile a minute, and my breath came out in hefty puffs. I didn't know where I was. I'd never seen this place before. White ceilings, white walls, bright fluorescent lights – where was I? A hospital?

A shadow suddenly hovered over me. Throwing myself back against the pillows, I pushed against the thin mattress, trying to escape from whatever stood above me. My lungs hurt, like they were collapsing. My arms and legs thrashed wildly. I had no control over my body. A mask of some sort was placed over my nose and mouth, leaking oxygen into my senses.

"Give her a little more," a male voice spoke. "She needs rest."

Right after those words were spoken, a cool feeling flowed through my veins. A few seconds went by. The spasms slowly ebbed away, my eyelids growing heavier. Once again I found myself fading away.

The Messenger

I watched the two sisters through the glass window of the door. Justine was struggling. Jenny knew it. Every moan, groan, cry, and muscle spasm that coursed through Justine broke Jenny's heart. She hated seeing her sister suffer, but she was so happy to have found her. She just wished she could ease her sister's agony.

Jenny knew God was in control, but couldn't abate the feeling of helplessness that became wrapped around her heart. Finding her sister proved that prayer produced miracles. This had God's hands all over it. Beautiful, guiding fingertips leading the way to future redemption.

Right now Jenny had her head bowed, with her elbows placed on the bed next to Justine. She knew her sister was being tormented in her sleep. The drugs that imprisoned Justine for so many years were slowly exiting her body, and she was feeling the heat of their escape. An uphill battle awaited. This would either make or break Justine.

Jenny knew all this. She'd seen it before. The way an addict was forced to experience unrelenting stress as they detoxed their systems. All the failures, all the triumphs, were fresh in her mind right now. Not only was she aware of the battle Justine's body and mind were going through, but she also knew of the demonic spirit attacking her while she attempted to rest.

Most people called Jenny a religious fanatic, a weirdo, your common "Bible Thumper", but to fellow believers she was known as a Prophet. God delivered words and visions to her. Basically, she was one of His interpreters.

Sometimes God allowed her to see in the spirit realm, giving her sight to both angelic and demonic beings. At this particular time, however, she wasn't able to see Satan's minion right in front of her. It wasn't time for her to see. Not yet.

Pharmakeia was his name. I'd known him before the fall. He had been a beautiful singer, and a trumpet player. Now he was a diseased entity, a distorted, wrung-out image of his former self.

Shaking my head, I continued to observe his blistered, jaundiced-colored hands reaching as far as they could inside Justine's body – one hand placed in her chest, the other in her head, injecting as much venom as he could to keep her in Hell's clutches. He had been by her side ever since the night her mother kicked her out. The mother had thought by kicking her out she'd have more of a chance, a way to escape the man who constantly broke her spirit.

Regrettably, her way of thinking had been greatly warped. Unknowingly, she had thrown her own flesh and blood to the wolves, the shadows immediately claiming the lost child. She'd also signed her own death warrant, which guaranteed her an eternity in Hell.

Pharmakeia, with a vicious grin on his morbid face, pushed more dark affliction into Justine's body, causing her to writhe and cry out in her sleep. Black ooze slid from sores on his skin, splashing and soaking into Justine's pores. No doubt her nightmares felt real. His hand was buried deep in her heart. The pain had to be excruciating.

With her sister's recent outburst, Jenny prayed even harder.

"When will we be able to intervene?"

Turning my attention to the right, I peered into a pair of glowing eyes, one blue, one green. Her name was Rachel, a fellow angel. A guardian over mankind.

Shifting my gaze back to the sisters I answered, "When He gives the go ahead. You know as well as I do that The Almighty is a gentleman. He will not force anyone to do what they do not want. Freewill has been established; it is up to Justine."

I heard her sigh next to me. "This is just the beginning of her suffering. If she could only see the monster levitating above her."

"God may give her sight, but for now she is blind." I contemplated that thought. "However, her dreams are revealing a lot to her right now. Pharmakeia's hard work could prove futile. He may be helping Justine by tormenting her."

"How so?" Rachel marveled curiously.

Looking back at her I replied, "The Dark is so intent on taking God's children, they sometimes, how should I say, *overwork* themselves. Like right now, Satan's little minion is forcing Justine to relive her horrendous past. Once she opens her eyes and sees Jenny, maybe she'll come to realize that her life can be different. That everything she's gone through isn't for nothing. That God brought her out of darkness so she can help others do the same."

"Or," Rachel added, "she'll wake up traumatized and angry at God. She may question why her life has been troubled, while her sister grew up in light and comfort. She may wonder why God let the chains of darkness incarcerate her for so long."

"Perhaps," I mused, gazing back through the window. "If she can get through the next few weeks, if Jenny can minister and show her how infinite God's love and grace is, then maybe Justine can become fully healed." I paused. "We have yet to know what His plans are. In the meantime, we wait. We wait for word to intervene."

"He's hearing Jenny's prayers," she told me. "He will reveal to her what she needs to know."

"Yes," I whispered. "But until then, we wait."

The Usher

I watched the two angels conversing with one another from the comfort of my office in Hell. How pitiful they were, thinking that this Justine could break the demonic stronghold that imprisoned her soul. It amused me that The Light thought they could just barge in and take back what rightfully belonged to Hell.

Ignorant little Celestials.

Pharmakeia was holding his own, despite the mortal

woman's prayers. I wasn't near the woman, but I could hear every word she spoke. Her words of faith was giving me a headache. With Pharmakeia being so close to one of the Almighty's saints, I could only imagine the torture he was going through ... well, maybe I *could* imagine.

Why did The Light want this soul? She was broken, damaged beyond repair. A used-up nobody.

Was it because of the sister, this Jenny? Yes, that had to be it. I'd seen her name several times on Hell's Most Wanted list. Word had been going around that she was a force to be reckoned with, given the power to see into the spirit realm and discern spirits. With her childlike faith and gifts, she'd saved many people from eternal damnation. She'd also sent a lot of my brethren away, using the Holy Spirit as her weapon to dislodge them from their assigned humans. My boss was not thrilled. Not at all.

The Light could try all they wanted, but Justine was ours. We'd worked too hard on keeping her in line. She was ours. If they wanted a battle, then so be it.

So. Be. It.

Chapter 3

Justine

"Justine," my mother whispered urgently. "Justine, wake up."

I sat up, rubbing sleep from my eyes. "Mama, what is it?"

"Get up and get your coat," she ordered, throwing a duffel bag into my hands. "You've got to leave. Now."

"What?" I asked, completely taken back. "What do you mean I have to leave?"

"It's for your own good," she replied, throwing my winter coat at me. "I've packed you a bag full of clothes and necessities. Go find a shelter as fast as you can."

"But Mama," I cried, with tears running down my cheeks, "I don't want to leave! This is my home – "

She grabbed my shoulders, gazing deeply into my eyes. "I know, Justine. I know what he does to you at night. I know he's a monster. He will not hurt you anymore."

For a moment I felt shame, embarrassed that she knew. My eyes slid to the floor, not wanting her to see the pain that shown from them. I didn't want her to see that I no longer held my innocence. The man she'd married had already stolen that from me. Her next words shook me to my soul's core.

"He will pay for hurting you, I promise."

Finding the courage to meet her eyes I inquired, "What about Jenny? I can't leave her."

Mom smiled, and for the first time I noticed the bruises that painted her face. It seemed that Ricky hurt her, too. Why hadn't I seen them before?

"Jenny will be fine," she assured. "She has God."

"What about us? Do we have God?"

Her smile faded, replaced with a frown. "God abandoned us, Justine. We're on our own."

I stared at her in disbelief, wondering how God could abandon us. Why would He do that? Were we not important enough to Him?

Why did He love Jenny more than us?

A car pulled up outside our apartment building. Ricky was home.

"Hurry!" Mom shrieked, pushing me toward the window. "Go down the fire escape and run, Justine. Run as fast as you can. Get as far away from here as possible!"

"But Mama!" I sobbed. "I don't want to go! I want to stay with you and Jenny."

She surprised me by pulling me into her arms and kissing the top of my head. Just as fast, she let go, her dark eyes peering into mine.

"Justine, I love you," she whispered, palming my cheek in her cold hand. "But you can't stay. You'll have more of a chance out there. If you stayed here, you would surely die."

The door to our apartment slammed open, shaking the windows. Both of us let out a cry. Mom shoved me out the window.

"Go, Justine."

"Mama, please..."

"Always remember I love you. I love you more than my life." She closed the window and pulled the blinds.

I climbed down the shaky metal ladder, crying the whole way.

Once my feet hit the pavement, I did what my Mama wanted. I ran. And ran ... and ran some more. It was dark, no moon or stars, just blackness, except for a few street lights. Tall buildings loomed in the dark, casting eerie shadows on the ground. Images of my little sister entered my mind. What would happen to her now? With me out of the picture, would Ricky snatch her out of bed and damage her? Just like he'd damaged me?

What about Mama? What would happen to her? Now that I was gone...

I ran until I couldn't take another step. Coming to a dirty alley, I slouched at its mouth, desperately attempting to catch my breath. My lungs were on fire. My feet felt covered in blisters. I was on my own, in this dark, cold city. Where was I to go? Where would I live?

"Hello. Do you need help?"

Gazing up, I stared into the green eyes of a young man, maybe seventeen or eighteen. He wore a pleasant smile on his face. Instantly I was drawn to him. I felt like I could trust him, which was weird since I'd never trusted anyone in my life. Well, ever since Ricky came into the picture.

"Yes," I sputtered out, standing up straight. "I need to find a shelter. My mom, she – "

"Kicked you out?" He interjected in an understanding tone.

I nodded, my face flushing with abashment.

"I know a place," he said, taking my hand in his. It was dirty and rough. "You want to come with me?"

"Yes," I answered, feeling a bit of relief.

"Good." He wiped at the tears falling down my face. "My name is Pete. What's yours?"

"Justine."

He grinned, this time a little savagely. "Well, Justine, welcome to my world."

With that he pushed me out of the alley, and into the arms of a pus-covered beast. Its elongated arms wrapped around me, lifting me off my feet so I was face to face with it. Its black eyes gazed into mine. A sinister smile touched his infected lips.

"Justine," it said, its voice sounding like nails on a chalkboard.

Fear snaked through my body, and I let out a bloodcurdling scream...

Waking up from my nightmare, the urge to throw-up hit me. Leaning over the side of the bed, I vomited, expecting a big splatter to hit the floor. Instead someone was there with a bowl. A soft hand pulled the hair from my face as I emptied my stomach.

A cool, wet towel was placed on the back of my neck. When my stomach became hollow, I continued to dry heave. This went on for a couple of minutes. My stomach cramped, hurting every heave my body produced.

Eventually the nausea subsided, and I laid back on the pillows, able to get a close look at the individual taking care of me. She had on jeans, a t-shirt, and wore her long blonde hair in a ponytail.

"Here," she said, holding out a cup of water. "Sip it, don't chug."

"Thank you." I took the water and sipped, relishing the cool liquid gliding down my dry throat. She smiled, a very pretty smile.

"You are welcome."

"Where am I?" I asked after three more sips, feeling a bit better.

The young woman stared at me with sincere blue eyes. "You're in a private rehab facility. You were brought in five days ago. We've been feeding you intravenously the last two days. "

My eyebrows shot up. "*Five days*! How is that possible?" I racked my brain, trying to remember where I'd been five days ago. The diner, Don sharing food, me sharing with my friend, her sharing...

"My friend," I bolted upright in bed, which caused stars to shoot behind my eyelids and my head to thump along with my heartbeat. Closing my eyes and laying back down, I questioned, "My friend. Is she here too?" The young woman hesitated before replying, prompting me to open my eyes. A sad expression painted her face.

"No, she's not." She sat down in the chair next to my bed, leaning her elbows on her thighs. "Did you know her name? Where she lived? Where she was from?"

I shook my head. "No – well, I think her name is Candy or Carrie ... wait, did you say *lived*? Did something bad happen?" The look on her face said it all.

"Justine, your friend is dead. From an overdose." She paused a moment, as if to gauge my reaction before continuing on. "We found the two of you together. You were highly doped, and she was already gone."

"Oh."

I wanted to be sad. I really did. But physical pain had me in a vise grip. All I could think about was the pain ... and how I needed it to stop. What I wanted was an escape.

"Justine, are you okay?"

She brought my attention back to her. I had not realized that I'd zoned out. Searching her over I saw the concern in her expression. What I didn't understand was why she held so much interest in me. I was a street person, a user, a boozer. I was nothing.

"How do you know my name?" I questioned, curious as to why I'd been brought here in the first place. She sighed, glancing down at her entwined hands placed in her lap.

A brief moment went by before she responded, "I've been searching for you a long time, Justine. I was too little to understand when and why you left, but now, after finding you, I feel we've been given a chance to reconnect." She continued to stare at her hands, transfixed on them. Maybe she was nervous.

"That doesn't really answer my question," I pointed out. That's when she made eye contact with me.

"Justine, it's me. Jenny. Your little sister."

Her response caught me off guard. This beautiful girl couldn't be my sister. Her skin was flawless, her clothes clean, her teeth perfectly straight – she even smelled like flowers on a summer day. She looked nothing like me – of course I'm sure my appearance had seen better days. I hadn't paid attention to my reflection in years.

After a moment of staring in her eyes, memorizing every detail on her face, I came to one important realization. This *was* my little sister. This *was* Jenny. An image of her ten year old self ran across my mind. The woman before me was an older version of the smiling, optimistic ten year old I'd known long ago.

"Jenny," I whispered, with big fat tears rolling down my cheeks. "It's really you."

Jenny

A gasp of surprise eluded my lips when Justine jumped from the bed, wrapping her long, skinny arms around my neck. Her body shook with raw, gut-wrenching sobs, maybe from jubilance, maybe from her body detoxing, I wasn't sure. I knew this was a sensitive time for her, an extremely confusing situation. When someone passes out and wakes up in an unknown place, they're bound to feel a little uneasy. Not to mention the fact that the person who found her was her long lost sister. If it were me, I'd definitely feel a bit of discomfort. Maybe a little bewilderment, too.

Since I'd started working for the center I'd come in contact with hundreds of homeless people and drug addicts. Some came to us willingly, wanting so badly to be free of the chains the devil held them in. Others, like Justine, came in all jacked up on drugs, stuck in their own personal hells that seemed endless. They didn't know that coming into the center was the easiest step of all. The steps that followed would prove how strong they were. The next steps were the absolute hardest.

"You're okay," I said softly, stroking her hair – I'd been able to get rid of her lice while she'd slept. "I'm going to make sure you get all the care you need."

I held onto her until she wore herself out. She laid back down and I covered her up, hoping the blanket would ease the chills she was experiencing. Walking over to the sink, I took a brand new washcloth and wet it, wringing out the excess water. Taking the back of my hand, I felt her forehead. She was burning up, so I placed the cool cloth on her bare skin. A sigh sounded from her lips.

"Thank you," she said, looking up at me with wet, glazed eyes.

I nodded, inquiring, "Do you need anything else?"

"Only one thing."

"What's that?"

Her eyes narrowed. "Is Mom okay? The night she kicked me out, she ... wasn't herself. I just need to know if she's okay."

A deep, unrelenting sadness squeezed my heart. It had taken me years to push that night out of my mind. Nightmare upon nightmare had held me prisoner for many years. I'd been young, weak, and impressionable. The enemy had used that time to harass me.

For a full straight year I'd felt unwanted, unloved, and worthless. That is, until I asked Jesus into my heart. When that happened, I had the ability to fight back and break the chains that had me tied down for so long.

I'd spoken of that night before, my personal testimony, using it as my ministry to help some afflicted by domestic abuse. As much as I hated talking about it, I knew it had to be done. Justine needed to know the truth.

Before I began, I inwardly prayed for God's guidance; for the right words to say.

"I don't know how to tell you this, but..." I sat down next to her. "Mom's dead, Justine. She's been dead for twelve years.

The night she kicked you out was the night she shot Ricky, and then herself."

Her eyes widened. "Mom's *dead*?"

"Let's wait until tomorrow to finish – "

"No!" She quickly sat up, throwing the washcloth to the ground. "I was kicked out for a reason, and I deserve to know why."

"She thought she was protecting you, Justine – protecting us!" I exclaimed. The next words out of my mouth came in a tidal rush. "I was young, but I knew what he was doing to you. I also knew that I would have been next. You see, Mom told me everything. She told me that Ricky was evil and hurting you. She told me that she was going to do something so you and I both would be safe. She told me to hide deep in my closet so he couldn't find me, because if he did find me, he would kill me.

"I heard everything, Justine. The arguing, the fighting, it bled into my bedroom. He broke down my door, searching for me, calling my name. He was intoxicated and ready to hurt someone, and since you were gone I was his new target. He threatened Mom, explaining every perverted thing he planned to do to me. That's when I heard the gun shot."

She stared at me, her mouth agape, as I allowed my memories to pour from my mouth. "I heard as his body fell to the ground, falling right in front of the closet door. I listened as Mom plopped down on the bed, sobbing, saying that she was sorry over and over again. Then she ... turned the gun on herself. Another shot blasted. She killed herself with one shot to the head."

I stood to my feet and walked across the room, my arms crossed at my chest. The memories, the horrid images that had been seared into my brain, was beginning to get to me. Tears of sadness and anger brimmed my eyes. Quickly I wiped them away so she wouldn't see the hurt there. I needed to be strong. *She* needed me to be strong.

When I was able to compose myself, I walked back over to her and sat down. Her eyes, wide and unblinking, were congested with incredulity, with silent tears dripping down her face. I had to get it together, for her sake. And mine.

"Justine, I'm sorry." I gently took her hand. "Mom thought it was the only way to save you, to save the both of us. It was wrong of her to kick you out. It was wrong of her to kill Ricky, and to kill herself. It was wrong. And she's paying for it."

She cocked an eyebrow. "What do you mean by that? How is she paying for what she did?"

"She killed him," I replied. "And then she killed herself. It was wrong, and she's in Hell for it." Shock rattled through my system when she busted out in an abrasive cackle.

"Oh, please, Jenny! Don't tell me you believe in that God junk." She shook her head. "Those were just bedtime stories we were told so we would stay in line. And besides, if there's really a God, why didn't He protect me from that monster? Why, Jenny, would He allow the abuse that me and Mom suffered through? It doesn't make sense. Not at all."

I prayed a silent prayer, then said, "God is real. He has a reason for everything. He has a plan for everyone. We are not promised an easy life, and with all the evil in this world the only one we can call out to is Jesus."

Justine's eyebrows shot up. "Okay, with that being said, let me ask you this: Why did, twelve years ago, He allow me to be thrown out in the streets to fend for myself? What did that accomplish? And not only that, why was it me? Why did I get thrown out, while you didn't?" She stared at me through narrowed eyes, her tone rugged and harsh. "That doesn't seem fair to me. If there really is a God, then I don't want any part if it. He's already shown how much He cares for me. Little to nothing, I guess. Little to nothing."

The room became silent. She rolled over on her side, her back facing me, and cried softly. I sat in my chair, running our conversation through my head. With being raped over and over again, then thrown out to the streets, I could almost see her unbelief. Thankfully, I had been spared that life. God had saved me from that situation by having an aunt and uncle raise me. I had never thought about why He had saved me from the life Justine was forced to lived.

I did know the truth, though. God was real, and so was Satan. Heaven and Hell was real, as well. It all came down to faith. I had enough faith to believe in the unseen, to understand that a spiritual war was being fought, even in the very room Justine and I were in. At this very second. I could feel it in the air, but at the moment I couldn't see it. Eventually the veil would be lifted from my eyes, giving me an edge. I'd seen angels before; I'd seen demons, too. Their presences were both accounted for at the moment. I knew this without seeing. When it was time, I'd see.

After all, I was a Seer. A Prophet. Visions and dreams were given to me by God Himself. I was His servant, and I trusted Him completely. There was a reason we'd found Justine. There's always a reason. But I didn't know the plan. It wasn't meant for me to know. At least, not right now.

Right now I just wanted my sister saved. *Completely* saved.

117

****

"Jenny! Jenny! Wake up!"

I jumped out of bed, switching on my lamp. Matching the voice with the face I asked, "Chase, what's wrong?"

"It's Justine, " he replied promptly.

That was all he had to say. I threw on my robe, tying it around my waist, and followed close behind him. We raced down the hall where a crowd had formed around an opened door. I could hear Justine's wailing, her screams echoing throughout the hallway. When we approached the scene, two nurses were trying to hold her down. Justine was half in, half out of the janitor's closet.

One of the nurses said, "We heard the screams from our station and found her in a fetal position. We can't get her calm!"

"Let her go!" I instructed. They did as they were told. I dropped to my knees and dragged her onto my lap. It was a hard feat to accomplish, but after whispering encouragement in her ear, she finally settled down. Her eyes opened and gazed into mine. I pushed sweaty strands of hair off her face, then clutched her to my chest.

That's the moment I saw it. The demon tormenting her.

I'd seen this abomination before. It harassed every addict that walked in the doors of the facility. Long arms and legs, diseased-looking skin – I could smell the rot and decay flowing off of him.

"*Pharmakeia*," a voice whispered in my ear. An angel's voice.

Narrowing my eyes, I looked at the demon and firmly spoke, "I rebuke you in the name of Jesus!"

Its expression turned into horror, bellowing in pain as it disappeared.

Chase knelt down beside me and asked, "What did you see?"

"A demon named Pharmakeia," I answered promptly. Chase just stared at me. He knew I was telling the truth. He knew how I was wired.

As I held Justine in my arms, I felt a huge weight lift off of me. I knew its name. I knew we could fight this. It was all up to Justine now. She'd have to want to get better. She'd have to decide to come to Jesus. On her own. No one could do it for her.

It was all up to her now.

Chapter 4

Justine (Two Weeks Later)

Despite wanting, needing, *craving* my next fix, I had decided to stay in rehab. My reasons were a little selfish. Hot showers, three meals a day, and a warm bed to sleep in at night – those three essential things alone were enough for my agreement to start rehabilitation. My sister, Jenny, was another reason I stayed.

We were spending a lot of time together, sometimes in the cafeteria, sometimes in my assigned room (which had its own bathroom). I'd learned that she was a nurse, being employed by the private rehab center. The three weeks I'd been here she was my nurse, day in and day out. When she wasn't on the clock, most of her time was spent on the streets, ministering to the homeless and helping them as much as possible. She'd told me that when I felt comfortable, I could join her and the others when they went out.

In many ways my little sister was a saint, which left me wondering how in the world we shared the same blood. The two of us were just so different.

When I decided to stay, I thought getting off drugs would be simple, especially with all the support I had. Boy, was I wrong. So wrong it was completely laughable. The pain that came with detoxing my body was indefinable. My muscles would spasm suddenly, my stomach sometimes felt like it was twisting inside itself ... simply a very unpleasant existence. But I could handle the physical discomfort better than I could the hallucinations. The waking nightmares were the worst part.

They felt so real, the hideous dreams. Most of them revolved around Pete, the first person I had met on the streets at the age of fourteen. He was the one that drew me into the drug world, giving me my first taste of hypnotic chaos.

Most of my dreams centered around my dead step-dad and a monster so malformed that no words could describe it. Sometimes they chased me down darkened paths and hallways, mocking me with their evil snarls and groping hands. A couple of times, during the second week, I'd been found lying in the hall (most recently the janitor's closet), pulled into a fetal position on the cold, dirty floor.

The psychiatrist I'd been seeing (his name was Eddie) had said sleepwalking was very common during detox, but I felt there was something more to it. It felt like Ricky and the monster had been in the room with me, while I was wide awake. I'd felt hands grabbing my arms, legs, and feet. Like I was living an awakened reality, instead of sleeping.

During group sessions I'd learned I wasn't the only one who suffered from sleepwalking. Mandy, one of the ladies from my group, had suffered it for three months. Her drug of choice had been cocaine, and when she'd began the detox her nightmares had grown with such intensity she couldn't differentiate between reality and fantasy. Monsters would crawl all over the ceiling and walls, looking like black shadows. People that hurt her from the past would also show up, taunting her, but they were never really there. For months she suffered this agony, until one night she'd had enough. She gave her life to God, asking Jesus into her heart. By doing this she let go of her past sinful life, trading it for a new, brighter one.

Mandy had insisted the monsters in her room were demons, because once she let go of that life and gave her heart to Jesus, they were gone.

Jenny and Mandy shared the same logic. These extremely real nightmares I experienced seemed to prove to Jenny that there was an unearthly force causing my sleep to be disturbed. A demonic entity, which sounded entirely absurd to me. She remained serious as a heart attack when I'd laughed in her face. I mean, please, a demon? A demon inflicting me? That only happened in horror movies and books.

"Jenny, I don't believe in all that mumbo-jumbo," I'd expressed very plainly to her.

With a stone cold expression she had replied, "When you're ready to face the truth, He will lift the veil from your eyes."

Now as I made my way to the cafeteria to have lunch with Jenny, I couldn't help but ponder those words. What did she mean about a veil lifting from my eyes? And more importantly, did I *want* to know the truth?

Walking through the cafeteria doors, I saw Jenny sitting at our usual table, where a huge plate-glass window overlooked a peaceful garden full of various flowers, trees, and plants. The Japanese Maple trees were my favorite. The sun shone through them, casting dancing shadows through the window. I sat out there many days, listening to the birds chirping, and wondered where my life was heading. Still didn't have that answer.

Jenny stood up and gave me a tight hug, her floral perfume and herbal shampoo gliding up my nose.

"Hey, you're looking so much better," she expressed as she let me go and took her seat. "Thanks for meeting with me. I've got about thirty minutes until my break is up."

Taking the seat across the table I pointed out, "Hey, anytime pizza is involved, I'll be here."

Jenny laughed. "Me, too!"

A large pepperoni pie sat in between us. At the same time we picked up a piece each, taking huge bites out of the greasy goodness. We sat their in silence, except for the sound of our chewing. I savored every bite I took. It was almost surreal that I was sitting in a clean cafeteria, eating yummy pizza with my little sister. Three weeks had passed, three hard but awesome weeks. I couldn't help but feel that this moment was precious, and that it could be snatched away at any moment. Like my friend that died next to me on the street. Carrie had been her name. One minute we were flying high, and the next minute...

"Is it good?" questioned Jenny, who watched as I grabbed a second piece.

I grinned. "You know, it's a bit crazy, but I've been here

almost a month and I've gained at least five pounds."

"That's a good thing," said Jenny, adding, "though you need to gain at least fifteen more, if you ask me."

"Maybe." I chomped off a cheesy bite, declaring, "Wow, this is so good!"

Smiling, Jenny marveled, "Better than anything on the streets, right?"

I sipped some water, then replied, "Definitely, though I still have cravings ... not as much as before, but they show up at certain times."

"Do the cravings hit you after your nightmares?"

I shrugged my shoulders. "Most of the time, yes."

"How is that going? The dreams, I mean. What are they about?"

A shiver tickled down my back. "The dreams are very ... realistic."

"How so?" She rested her elbows on the table, dropping her chin onto her balled-up fist. When I didn't answer directly she said, "If you don't want to talk about it, we don't have to."

"No, it's fine," I assured her, placing the half-eaten slice on my paper plate. "This can count for my therapy today."

Jenny laughed. "Okay, I can handle that."

Grinning, I sucked in a deep breath and let it out slowly. I told myself that I needed to talk to someone, to get this craziness out of my bruised mind. Might as well be my little sister. She seemed to understand the madness when I did not.

"The other night, after you left, I got ready for bed. Took a shower, brushed my teeth, and slid under the covers. I turned off my lamp and was about to close my eyes, when I saw someone standing in front of the door. I turned on the light, thinking you might have come back, but it ... it..." My heart began to speed up, the memory of that night beginning to trigger a panic attack. Closing my eyes, I took deep breaths, hoping to squelch the attack I knew was building. The touch of Jenny's hand wrapping around mine helped to ease the anxiety.

"Go ahead," she murmured. "You're safe. Nothing can hurt you, I promise."

Opening my eyes, I nodded and continued with my story. "Ricky stood there. Plain as day. He locked eyes with me. His expression was of anger. He let out a cry and started sprinting toward me. That's when I pinched my eyes closed and waited for, I don't know ... impact or something. After a few seconds passed, and he hadn't barreled into me, I opened my eyes. Ricky was gone, but something else stood in his place. It stood at the end of my bed, staring at me through blackened eyes."

Tears began to build in my eyes as my body started to shake uncontrollably. Sweat trickled down my neck and back. The image that had become seared in my brain was worse than any horror movie monster I'd ever seen. It had looked so real, so substantial, causing me to question my sanity. How could my mind create such a hideous anomaly?

"Justine," Jenny said. Her tone was serious as she stared at me. "What was it? Describe it to me."

I softly replied, "A monster, covered with sores and boils. It was only visible for two or three seconds. Long enough for me to think I'm crazy."

An understanding expression painted her face as she asked, "Anything else?"

I nodded. "A smell. I can't even begin to describe it. It smelled like..."

"Death and decay," she said, finishing my sentence.

I shot her a questionable look. "Yeah – how did you know?"

"Because I've seen it. I've smelled it." Her eyes narrowed. "And I loathe it."

Taken back by her answer I expressed, "I don't understand..."

"Justine," she uttered slowly, "what I'm about to tell you may seem a little out of the ordinary for you. But I can promise that every word I speak is truth." She paused, giving me a chance to speak, but I had nothing to give, so she continued. "We've gotten to know each other again. We're able to be sisters again, and I give all the glory to God. Me finding you, and us being together, is a miracle. A God-produced miracle. A prayer answered. And before you say anything, I know how you feel about God, but let me ask you this – Are you ready to hear the truth?"

I raised my eyebrows, unsure I wanted to hear what she would be saying next. "I guess so."

"You've got to keep an open mind."

"I'll try." She shot me a stern look, so I added, "Really, I will!"

"Okay," she breathed out, appearing satisfied by my words. She continued on. "The enemy is attacking you in your dreams. The enemy is Satan. The monster you saw – the tall, malformed, smelly being – is a demon. One of Satan's soldiers."

"Jenny..." I began, shaking my head. She ignored me and went on.

"Its name is Pharmakeia, and I've seen it many times before. Its targets are the homeless, alcoholics, drug addicts – it uses persuasive traits to lure the lost and broken down a destructive path. And now that you've decided to get clean, the enemy has ordered it to make your life a living nightmare. It knows your weaknesses, it knows your hurts. That's why Ricky and Pete are in your dreams, taking you back to a time where you had no choice."

"So, you're saying," I stated, "that the devil, whom I don't believe exists, is torturing me in my sleep, using our rapist of a step-dad, a drug dealer, and a stinky demon to get the job done."

Sighing she replied, "Yes, but I'm not finished yet."

"Oh, please continue!" I cackled, crossing my arms at my chest. "Your stories are freakishly amazing. You should be a writer!" I glared angrily at her, disbelieving that my sister would play these stupid games with me.

"They are more than just stories," she said, her tone

chillingly serious. Sitting straighter in her seat, she proceeded forward. "Let me take you back to the night you were kicked out twelve years ago. You see, not only did your life change that night, but so did mine."

My heart stuttered in my chest. Clearing my throat I urged, "Go right ahead."

"I heard Mom talking to you that night. I heard the anguish in her voice when she told you to leave. At the time, I'd wanted to run in your room and hold on to you, but my body was frozen. I couldn't move. Not until I heard a voice whisper for me to hide in the closet."

"You said Mom told you to hide," I pointed out, remembering our first conversation. "How could she have told you that while she was with me?"

"Because," Jenny softly uttered, "Mom wasn't the one who had said it."

A huge boulder of perplexity fell on top of me, pushing me to inquire, "Then who did? God?" I laughed a little at that last word.

She didn't laugh. Instead she answered, "Sort of. You see, that night was the night God blessed me with a gift that I use to this day."

"Oh yeah?" My voice was on the snarky level. "And what gift would that be?"

She leaned her elbows on the table and stared me right in the eye.

"The gift of a Seer."

The Usher

"You wanted to see me, Master?"

I turned around to see Pharmakeia standing in a corner. His smell radiated around the room, but I chose not to point that out. The situation was just too dire.

"Yes, Pharmakeia, and I appreciate you arriving on schedule." Pharmakeia nodded his head. I continued. "You need to go to Justine right now."

Cocking his head to the side he retorted, "But she is the same. She doesn't believe anything her sister says. I've been whispering lies in her ear, I've been plaguing her dreams with her deplorable past – "

"Her sister knows your name."

His back hit the wall, his expression floored. "How is that? I know she saw me and she commanded me to leave, but she didn't say my name."

"The Messenger, Gabriel," I enlightened him. "He whispered in her ear. That's how she knows."

Pharmakeia slumped his shoulders, his blistered lips forming into a frown. This was bad. This was *really* bad. When a servant of the Most High had the gifts of a Prophetic Seer, with the Holy Spirit living within them, it made it really hard for demons to possess and badger humans. Unless said humans didn't want anything to do with the good side, using their freewill to ignore the signs of the holy ones. If that was the case, the Seer could try all they wanted and it wouldn't make a bit of difference. If the one they were trying to help didn't let go of their troubled past, it kept the door open for more iniquity to enter their lives.

However, Justine was about to remember her life before Ricky entered it.

"Your orders, Master?" Pharmakeia asked, standing tall and attempting to be brave. The idiot. Fear blew off of him as strong as tornadic winds. I chose not to say anything about his forced courage.

Time was of the essence. We were running out of it.

"Go to Justine now," I directed. "She is in the presence of her prophetic sister, and is about to be taken down memory lane, back to a time where it was just herself, her mother, and sister. A time without a stepfather – you understand?"

"Yes, I do." Before he disappeared he wondered, "What are you going to do?"

"I'm going to find Justine's first friend on the streets." A smile graced my lips. "I'm going to find Pete."

Chapter 5

Jenny

I watched as Justine scrunched up her nose. She shot me a strange look, with a brief glimpse of shock and disbelief. This would have to be brought out delicately and precise. I was about to explain what exactly happened that horrible night; I was about to let her in on the gift God gave me.

"A Seer," she finally spoke after a few silent seconds.

I nodded. "Yes, though in the Holy Bible the word Seer changed to Prophet."

Matching my movements, she placed her elbows on the table, resting her chin on top of her closed fists. "Tell me – what does all that entail?"

"I'm one of God's interpreters." With her eyebrows stitching together with puzzlement, I went on to explain. "It means that God speaks to me, sometimes through visions, sometimes through dreams. He also sends angels my way, messengers to whisper in my ear. And sometimes, not all the time, but some, He allows me to see into the spirit realm. When He allows me to see into the world that is unseen to most humans, I'm able to witness angels and demons.

"That's how I was able to see the demon in the janitor's closet. God allowed me to see what was afflicting you, and a messenger angel whispered its name into my ear."

She looked at me through stormy eyes. "Why are you doing this to me? You know that I don't believe in this junk. And nothing you say to me will change my mind. *Ever.*"

I took a deep breath, and inwardly prayed that what I was about to say would open her eyes. I prayed that she would wake up and see the truth.

The Messenger

Pharmakeia was back in all his disgusting, putrid glory. He stood behind Justine, though his eyes were fixed on me. An evil grin slowly crept across his diseased lips. Jenny couldn't see him at the moment, and the demon knew it.

"Hello, Messenger," Pharmakeia grated out, his voice like

nails on a chalkboard.

"Pharmakeia," was all I said back. It was pointless to carry on a conversation with him. Completely pointless. However, that didn't stop him from running his mouth.

"It appears that the Seer can't *see* me," he brazenly mocked, shifting his gaze to the sisters. "I've heard this one is going to tell a little story in hopes of convincing Justine to join The Light. I can't let that happen. You see, Justine has been my little pet for years. She belongs to me. She belongs to my lord, Satan. Do you have anything to say to that, Messenger?" When I didn't respond, he kept up his irritating banter, letting loose a mirthless cackle. "Yes, this one is already registered in Hell. Why, you may as well give up!"

I crimped my eyes at him and whispered, "Never."

Another bark of laughter eluded him. "We shall see."

Ignoring his decomposing presence, I concentrated all my attention on the two sisters. Jenny was telling her side of the story the night Justine was forced onto the streets. The entire truth.

"That night I saw my first angel," Jenny informed Justine, her eyes tearing up a bit. "A glorious angel from Heaven. She was so indescribably beautiful, and when she took my hand I felt

God's love and comfort flow through my body, instantly erasing the fear that had me frozen.

"A glow radiated off her, a bright white light that lit the way to the closet. Her bright blue, almost clear eyes had peered down at me, and she said, 'Follow me, Jenny, and God will protect you'. And that's exactly what God did. He had protected me from the horrors that took place in my bedroom that night."

Pharmakeia leaned into Justine's ear and whispered, "Why didn't He protect *you*, Justine? Why didn't He send an angel to protect you from the horrors you experienced? You must not be as special as Jenny."

Justine squirmed in her seat as his voice echoed in her head. Not knowing of his presence, she no doubt thought those words were her own. I could feel the anger building inside her, roiling and churning like the sea during a hurricane. Unfortunately, I couldn't do or say anything ... *yet*. Freewill was in place. This was Justine's fight.

Jenny continued speaking as her mind traveled back in time, not realizing that Pharmakeia was busy spreading poison through Justine's head.

"She guided me to the closet," Jenny softly spoke, "and we both hid together underneath mounds of clothing and blankets. I laid my head on a huge teddy bear, using its plush body as a pillow. She wrapped her warm, glowing arms around me and sang hymns, soothing me with her angelic voice. In the background I could hear Mama and Ricky screaming at each other, but my focus stayed on the angel. Even when the shooting occurred, she sang, the whole time staring into my eyes, keeping me transfixed..."

Pharmakeia laughed in Justine's ear, declaring, "She's such a pathetic liar! An angel saved her? *God* saved her? Bah! She's so stupid, maybe insane since she believes in that *Creator* nonsense! Heaven and Hell doesn't exist! She's such an idiot. Why are you listening to her? Why are you still here?" He lifted his eyes and glared at me, grinning from ear to ear. Black slime oozed from his mouth.

"I fell asleep in the angel's arms," Jenny continued, a smile tugging at her lips. "The police found me the next morning, underneath the piles of clothing and blankets, sound asleep on the closet floor."

Justine's face had turned beet red, her eyes filled with rage. The thoughts Pharmakeia was pouring through her mind was getting to her. All the lies, questions, *everything* the diseased entity spoke had pierced into Justine's heart, and now she was more perplexed as ever. Jenny gasped when Justine suddenly jumped up, the plastic chair she'd been sitting in flipping to the floor.

"Justine—"

"Stop!" shouted Justine. All heads in the cafeteria quickly shifted to the sisters, curious to what the disturbance implicated. Justine continued with, "I'm done listening to this junk about God loving you more than me."

Jenny's jaw dropped as she exclaimed, "That is not true! He loves you, Justine. He always has."

"If there was a God, you wouldn't have suffered," Pharmakeia whispered, still guiding her thoughts. "God doesn't exist."

"Yeah right!" scoffed Justine. Leaning down so as to get in Jenny's face, she added, "There is no God." She jerked back when Jenny stood up and walked around the table.

Standing shoulder to shoulder with her sister, Jenny asked, "Remember when we used to go to church? When it was just Mom, you, and I?"

"No," Justine countered, taking a step back. Jenny took a step forward.

"You were ten years old when you gave your live to

Jesus," Jenny told her, hoping she could still remember that part of her life. "I was only six, but I can remember that day like it was yesterday." Justine took another step back; Jenny stepped forward and pressed on. "There was an altar call, and you were the first one down. You professed that Jesus was your Lord and Savior, and asked Him to come into your heart."

"Lies, all lies!" Pharmakeia cried into Justine's ear. "That never happened! She is *lying!*"

Justine shook her head back and forth. An overwhelming wave of discomfort mixed with a storm of fury fell on top of her, rattling her system. It was hard for me to watch. I clenched my teeth together, biting my tongue so I wouldn't speak. I knew she was suffering, that she was confused and lost, but I couldn't do anything. I couldn't even stop Pharmakeia from messing with her mind. As much as I wanted to send him back to Hell, it wasn't time. God hadn't sent official word. Not yet.

Jenny reached out a hand, resting it on Justine's shoulders. "Don't you remember that day? Your face was all aglow ... you were *happy.*"

"It didn't last, did it?" Justine questioned. Her body trembled in complete vexation.

Jenny frowned. "No, because after that Mama met Ricky."

"He didn't bother me at first," Justine pointed out, with a faraway look in her eyes. "I actually liked him. Then a couple years later, it all changed."

"Hahaha, *yeah* it did!" remarked Pharmakeia as he rubbed his hands together. It took all I had to not pummel him into the ground. Inwardly I prayed that God would allow me to get that chance. Or at least see it happen.

"It did," agreed Jenny, her hand still on Justine's shoulder. "It all changed when he noticed that you were growing up. When he noticed you were changing into a woman, he changed as well, from father figure to rapist."

"Why did he hurt me?" Tears poured down Justine's cheeks as she gazed into her sister's eyes.

"Because he was wicked. A wicked human being."

Justine shook her head. "Why did God let him do that? Why didn't God save me?"

"God gave mankind freewill," Jenny responded lightly. "Ricky could have chosen to be a righteous, godly man, but he chose the opposite. He chose darkness, and he hurt you. And I'm sorry he hurt you, Justine. I'm so sorry."

"And the lies continue." Pharmakeia walked around

Justine, continuing his harmful whispers. "There is no way if God truly existed that this should have happened to you. She's flinging her deceit at you, trying to control you. Don't let her win, Justine. Don't let ... her ... *win*."

All of Justine's madness boiled over. She shrugged off her sister's hand and shoved her in the chest. Jenny, not foreseeing this change in events, was taken by surprise, her bottom hitting the hard cafeteria floor. Justine towered over her, with hands on her hips and a scowl on her face. People, patients and workers alike, began walking over to see what all the commotion was about.

"Enough lying, Jenny!" Justine permitted anger to control her words. "I'm done listening to your garbage! You think you're able to control me with this God nonsense. You actually expect me to believe that God sent an angel to protect you? Where was God the first night Ricky prowled into my room and took away my innocence? Where was he, Jenny?"

Jenny crawled back onto her feet and tried to protest, "Listen to—"

"No, listen to *me*!" Justine loudly interrupted. "I'll tell ya where he was, *little sister*. He wasn't there because *He* doesn't *exist*!"

With that last sentence, Justine stomped off, pushing through the small circle of people that had congregated around them. She stormed out the doors that led to the flower garden, slamming the door behind her. Whispers flew through the air, all eyes falling on Jenny, who had a crestfallen expression plastered on her face. I could hear her prayers, and I knew she wanted to run after her sister. Before she took one step, I placed a hand upon her shoulder.

"Let her go," I said softly, knowing she could hear me. Instead of following her sister, she turned around and ran into the ladies bathroom. When she was out of sight, the onlookers dispersed, though tongues were still wagging, all wondering what had just gone down. Cackling sounded to the left of me. I shifted my gaze to Pharmakeia. He had a superior expression on his pus-covered face. He grinned at me.

"That was too easy," he proclaimed, with his head shaking back and forth. "Humans lack any real smarts. They are all puppets, and my master is the puppeteer. Justine belongs to me. She belongs in Hell."

"You haven't won yet, demon." My body began to glow with Heaven's light, causing Pharmakeia's skin to burn. He quickly fled the scene. The light was too tortuous for him or any devil to stay around. Shifting my gaze to the sky, I prayed.

"Convict Justine's heart, Father," I softly sent up. "Help her to let go of the past. Make her remember You."

The ball was in Justine's court. It was up to her now.

Justine

I crashed through the doors that led to the garden, just as a sob escaped my chest. Tears of sadness, anguish, and anger flowed down my face, each tear a reminder of what I'd experienced in life. How could Jenny treat me that way? Why did she bring up the past, knowing that I was extremely unstable at the moment? I thought she loved me, but I guess I was wrong. If she could not except that I didn't agree with her religious views and her way of thinking, how would we ever get along?

We wouldn't be able to see eye to eye. Not with her strong convictions. She believed in it all – angels, demons, Heaven, Hell ... God. She even believed that she was a Seer, believing that God had given her the gift of seeing into a spiritual realm.

Craziness. Pure craziness. But then again, how was she able to describe the monster I'd seen in my room? How did she know about its stench?

Jenny had called it a demon. Its name was Pharmakeia. If there wasn't something to this God stuff, where did she get such a vivid imagination? Not only that, where did my illogical imagination come from?

I took a seat on a concrete bench situated next to a rock waterfall. The tranquil pitter-patter of the water hitting the rocks helped soothe my aching temples. The mid-afternoon sun bled through the Japanese Maples that littered this garden of serenity. I'd been coming here the last couple of weeks, using the time to think. To contemplate. The garden was the only place I felt safe. Secure. At peace. Though after the conversation with Jenny, my mind was twisted into a tight knot of confusion, with sadness weaved throughout.

I couldn't stay here. I didn't belong here. True, I wanted to get better. I didn't want a life on the streets anymore. I was even getting to a point where I didn't crave a hit. But I didn't belong here.

My thoughts swerved onto a different path. Jenny had brought up the day when I'd become saved, and every word she spoke was true. I had felt different when I'd gone down to the altar and prayed, asking Jesus into my heart. I felt wanted. I felt loved. But all that changed when Ricky appeared in our lives. With all he'd done to me, I'd lost all faith. God lost my trust. It had left me believing that He didn't exist. Deep down, though, I knew He did. What I couldn't understand is why He'd let me down. Why, with Him being a loving and all-knowing God, did He let me get hurt over and over again?

It didn't make sense to me. That's why I chose not to acknowledge His existence, because He had stopped acknowledging mine.

"Psst! Hey, Justine, over here!"

A voice caught my attention, breaking into my woeful thought train. A man stood at the chain-linked fence that surrounded the rehab center. One hand was clinging onto the fence, the knuckles appearing tensed and white. I couldn't see his face from where I sat, though the voice sounded vaguely familiar.

"Pete, is that you?" I called out. My heart tinkered out of control, bouncing around like a pebble in my chest. I didn't want to walk over to him. Something inside of me screamed to ignore the uninvited visitor. My feet, however, had a brain of their own.

Apparently.

As I meandered over to the fence, Pete's face became

clearer. He looked older than I remembered. His black hair had hints of gray, and he'd lost a lot of weight; he was half the person he used to be. Sharp cheekbones jutted out from his pale face. Dark circles inhabited the spaces underneath his eyes, which were bloodshot.

"Come on over here, Justine Baby," he urged, motioning with his hand. "Come to me."

Cautiously I walked up, stopping at the edge of the fence. He grinned, showing off his yellow teeth – a few of them were missing, most likely due to all the Meth he'd used in his life. I was lucky, because I still had all my teeth. He appeared not as lucky.

I got within one foot of the fence before his offensive smell hit me. Alcohol, cigarettes, and body odor all rolled into one.

"Um, Pete? What are you doing here? It's been years."

"Yeah, it's been a few." Taking a shaky hand, he ran it through his hair. His green eyes roamed me up and down. "Man, girl, you have grown up! How old are you now – nineteen? Twenty?"

I rolled my eyes. "Twenty-six."

"Right!" he exclaimed. "Twenty-six. Wow. Time sure does fly."

An uncomfortable silence passed between us, prompting me to ask, "Why are you here, Pete?"

"Well, I don't rightly know," he replied. A nervous laugh pushed out of his mouth. "I was just sitting at home, smoking a joint and chillin', when I heard a man say my name directly behind me. I'd jumped from my recliner, reaching for my baseball bat, but then stopped when I saw no one in the room with me.

"Anyway, I sat back down and lit me another one, when I heard the man's voice again. Only this time it was inside my head."

"In your head?" I curiously marveled.

"Yeah!" he readily answered, his head a big nod. "He told me exactly where you were and that you needed to see me, so, yeah ... here I am." I didn't say anything. All I could do was stare at him with my mouth agape, feeling complete disbelief on what his tongue was spouting. That's when he added, "Really! I'm telling you the truth. I'm not trippin'."

A large rock of dread hurled into my stomach. Standing just a foot from the man who gave me my first hit, I could feel the evil emanating from him – I could actually *feel* it! An unsettling presence drifted in the middle of us, and for a second I thought I saw a man-shaped shadow, followed by an eerie chill that caused goosebumps to blanket my skin. It only lasted a couple of seconds, but that was enough for me to want to get as far from him as possible.

About to close the conversation, I began to say, "Listen, Pete, I—"

"Wait!" he interrupted snappily. "He also said you were needing a hit – you know, the good stuff. And I got exactly what you need." Slowly, he reached into his pocket, sweeping his gaze to the left, then to the right, and pulled out two syringes.

Chapter 6

The Messenger

Justine's heart had sped up when Pete brought out the two syringes of Meth. I was disturbed at the scene unfolding before my eyes, and I was still awaiting orders from above. I wanted to yank Justine back, or at least send Jenny to her side, but I could not do that. Had to wait.

All I could do was watch Justine and Pete talk, but they weren't alone. Standing to the side of Pete was someone from long ago. I hadn't seen him in ages. Instead of robes of white and fluffy soft wings, he now wore a black robe, cinched around his waist. A hood covered his head. Red glowing eyes could be seen peeking out of the hood, along with a long nose and black lips, and skin a bright red. He usually stayed in the confinements of Hell, sending out lowly demons to do his dirty work. For whatever reason, he was here. Now. Being the puppeteer to his puppet.

His name used to be Zederich. A long time ago he orchestrated beautiful symphonies for the Lord. Now he worked for the dark prince, his occupation sending lost souls to their demented eternities. He was known as The Usher, the first entity that wicked souls met when they crossed the threshold of Hell.

The Usher didn't look at me, didn't even glance my direction. He was too concerned with the back and forth going on between the two humans, which caused me to shift my attention to the uneasy scene.

"Pete, I don't do that anymore," Justine informed him. Her eyes remained on the drugs in his hand.

"Your favorite, Justine." Pete grinned. The Usher whispered softly into his ear.

Justine was conflicted. On one hand, she wanted to take both syringes and shoot up so she could escape reality, maybe for good. Though on the other hand, she wanted to change – she wanted a real life change.

"No, Pete. I'm sorry. I'm not that girl anymore." Her voice trembled, but she stayed calm. I inwardly cheered her on, thankful the other hand won this situation.

Pete's smile disappeared. "There's another reason I'm here."

"What's that?" Justine breathed.

"I'm here to bust you out." Gently he placed the two syringes on the ground, then reached into his back pocket and pulled out a pair of wire cutters. He inspected the fence and saw where there was a hole of broken wire, big enough for an arm to fit through. That's where he began his sad attempt of breaking her out.

I watched in amazement as he worked and worked on cutting through the wire. It would be nightfall before he made any progress, but by then reinforcements would have him stopped.

I didn't foresee what happened next.

"Pete, stop!" exclaimed Justine. She moved closer to the fence, and as she did, Pete dropped the wire cutters to the ground. At the last second, it dawned on Justine what was about to happen, and she quickly turned around, ready to flee. She wasn't fast enough. His hand wrapped around her neck, yanking her back against the fence. I watched as he began to squeeze her neck.

Stepping forward, I was halted by The Usher's bantering chuckle.

"No, no, no," he taunted, wagging a red finger at me. "It is not yet time."

He was right. I was still waiting on orders from the Most High. But I didn't have to like it.

"Usher," I hissed through my teeth, "when this day is over, you will be burning in the lake of fire."

The Usher turned his red eyes on me, taking off his hood in the process. He looked so different. In Heaven he had been glorious, his beauty radiant and majestic. Now his skin was red and mottled, the golden brown hair he'd once had gone, leaving his head slick and bald.

"I don't think so," he grunted.

Please Lord, I prayed inwardly. *Give me word. Let me know what I am to do.*

That's when he answered me.

"Get the sister, the Prophet."

****

I found Jenny in the ladies restroom. She was standing in front of the sink, splashing water onto her face. Her puffy eyes and red nose spoke of a recent crying spell. Try as she might, the powder she was caking on her face would not hide the evidence of tears.

Leaning into her ear, I softly said, "Go to the garden. Justine needs you."

Jenny had heard me. She was startled for a moment, her eyes searching for the voice's body. But she couldn't see me; God's orders.

"Got it," she said aloud. With one last look in the mirror and a prayer, she ran out the doors of the bathroom. I was now alone.

Nodding my head I expressed, "Father, she is on the way. Time to rally up the troops."

And that's exactly what I did.

Justine

Pain slowly ebbed through my body as Pete squeezed harder around my neck. I clawed at his hand, digging my nails into his skin until I drew blood. But it was no use. He was stronger than me.

"Justine, you belong with me!" he cried. With each word he tightened his grip.

A stinging burn ignited my lungs as all the air I had left was forced out. Tears poured down my face. My ears popped. My eyes bulged. I tried to scream but couldn't make a sound. I couldn't breathe. I was dying. I knew it. So I stopped fighting.

Suddenly a bright light surrounded me as images started flashing before my eyes. A little girl wearing a white dress and pigtails, walking down to the altar at church. She dropped to her knees and clasped her hands under her chin in prayer. A group of churchgoers surrounded her as she recited the sinners prayer. She asked Jesus into her heart. At that moment, singing sounded throughout the congregation. Not only that, but angels wearing robes of white and pale wings appeared around the church. About five surrounded the little girl, all with raised hands and worshiping God.

Before I took my last breath, I realized that the little girl was *me*.

"L-Lord," I croaked out. "Ple-ease forgi-ive me."

I closed my eyes. That's when Jenny's voice rang through

the air.

"Let my sister go!"

Immediately Pete released me. I fell to my knees, coughing and gagging, trying to take in deep breaths. All the while I crawled on my knees, wanting to get as far away from the fence as possible. Arms wrapped around me. Footsteps slapped the pavement. I heard Jenny talking.

"Chase, take Justine inside. Get her checked out." She added softly, "Call the police."

"You got it," Chase said.

"Whoa!" I expressed when I was lifted off my feet. Opening my eyes I saw that Chase had picked me up.

"Justine," Jenny said. Her face popped up next to Chase. "Chase is going to get a doctor to check you out. Okay?"

I nodded. "Okay. Oh! And Jenny?"

"Yeah?"

"I've seen the light." I smiled lazily. "I believe now."

Jenny's eyes lit up and she laughed out loud. "That's great, Justine. We'll talk about it later."

I continued to smile as Chase began to carry me inside. My eyes didn't leave Jenny's until she was out of sight.

The Usher

An animalistic hiss sounded behind me. Pharmakeia was twitchy and spooked, and for a severe reason. The Prophet had arrived, armed with the Holy Spirit. Being in its vicinity sent tremors of fear to skitter down my spine – a feeling I wasn't used to. If I lost this soul to The Light, lord Satan would be extremely displeased. An agonizing punishment would await both Pharmakeia and I if we messed up. I couldn't allow that to happen.

"Your orders, master?" inquired Pharmakeia, his voice wavering.

I sighed, knowing there was only one thing we could do if we had any shot at winning this battle. There was two of us and only one Prophet. A *female* Prophet at that. This would be a piece of cake.

"My dear Pharmakeia. I think you know what we have to

do."

While the Prophet talked with Justine and the man, Pharmakeia and I dug our claws into Pete's body. Immediately I had taken over his body, and the Prophet would be speaking to me, not the human.

It was almost too easy.

Almost.

Chapter 7

Jenny

Happiness touched my heart at the good news Justine had just shared. A dense weight of sorrow lifted from my shoulders, my spirits soaring at full capacity. I watched as Chase took Justine inside. She still had that dreamy look in her eyes. It took me back to the day she asked Jesus into her heart. She'd held that same gaze when she was ten years old. I believed it when she said that she'd seen the light, and it made me want to dance and rejoice. But now wasn't the time. Not with Pete standing just outside the fence. Chase would be calling the police now, so I had little time to get down to business. I had to keep Pete here so the authorities could deal with him.

Slowly turning around, I was instantly aware that Pete wasn't alone. Standing next to him were two demonic beings, one I'd seen before, and one I hadn't seen. This new demon was wearing a long black robe. Its body was human-like, not a deformed monstrosity like Pharmakeia. The red-mottled skin, black lips, and black eyes that glowed red in the irises took the human part out of the equation. Oh, and the two horns protruding from its forehead – definitely not from this world.

Raw shivers attacked my system, but not because I was frightened. I was preparing for battle. I knew this because the hazy glare in Pete's eyes indicated that the demonic forces were controlling him.

Making direct eye contact, I held my head high, puffed out my chest, and, with no fear, marched over. I stopped a mere foot from the fence, which made the demons uneasy. They took a step back, pulling Pete's body with them. Obviously the demons loathed me. I already knew Pharmakeia felt that way. I'd sent it away a few times since I'd started work at the rehab center.

A sick feeling arose in my stomach. They had full control of him – Pete was their puppet, and my spirit became bristled. Agitated. Angry. *Provoked.*

Different smells wafted through the air. I couldn't tell if they were coming from Pete or the ones holding him hostage.

"Well, if it isn't the all powerful Seer," the demon with red skin spoke. Its eyes burned like orange-red coals. "I've heard about you. You have caused many disturbances in Hell."

"Let me talk to Pete," I ordered. I didn't want to waste my time talking to the enemy. I had to get through to Pete. Talk to him before the police did.

The red-skinned monster laughed. "Oh, Pete's a little busy right now—"

"I rebuke you, Pharmakeia, in the name of Jesus! Be gone!" I watched as the demon named Pharmakeia was ripped back, its claws dislodging from Pete's body. High-pitched screams flew from the demon's mouth as it vanished into thin air. No doubt, it was on the way to Hell. Or already there.

The robe-wearing demon still had Pete in its clutches. Taking a couple of steps back, it pulled Pete with it. A look of surprise spread across its face. Pete's eyes were glazed over, and his expression sat motionless. He had no idea that a demon held him captive. I had no doubt that if Pete could see what stood with him, he would change his life. No doubt.

"You can't get rid of me, Prophet!" the demon growled.

"Let him go!" I'd about had enough of this, my spirit enraged.

An arrogant smirk painted its ugly mug. "You can't tell me

what to do! I am The Us—"

I cut the monstrosity off. "Demon, I command you to release this man's body and leave, in the name of Christ Jesus!"

Shock and dismay replaced the arrogance in its expression as its claws became detached from Pete's shoulder. The force of separation caused Pete to fall forward on his knees.

"No!" the demon shouted. "It can't be! This can't—" It vanished before the sentence could be finished.

After the demon's vanishing act, a bright white light singed the air. When the light died down, I saw that angels, around ten or more, had circled around Pete and I. For a moment I was taken back by the wondrous sight. All dressed in white, I took in there feathery white wings and their outstretched hands. Their eyes were closed, their lips moving – they were all praying in a Heavenly language. It was music to my spirit.

Then, in the blink of an eye, they all disappeared, taking with them their beautifully scripted voices. Pete and I were the only ones left, along with the chorus of birds and nearby traffic.

Though the angelic beings were unseen, I could still sense their calming, warm presences lingering in the air. They were still here, only now located in the spiritual realm. God had sent in reinforcements. My valor soared; the same could be said for my spirit.

I dropped to my knees, coming face to face with Pete. Right in front of the man Justine had first met on the streets; the man who got her hooked on drugs. I was grateful there was a fence in between us, because if there wasn't I'd have been tempted to gift him with the same abuse he'd just shown Justine. Sometimes it was hard to turn the other cheek.

Extremely hard.

"Justine!" Pete sobbed, his hands yanking at his hair.

I loudly cleared my throat and said, "Pete. Look at me, Pete."

Sluggishly he lifted his head, meeting my eyes with his bloodshot ones. He looked disoriented, with a shock of confusion stitched into his expression. His eyes continued to soak in my face.

"You're not Justine," he finally said, his tone drenched in anger. He stood to his feet and put his face up to the hole he'd used to grab Justine. I matched his movements, unafraid of his defiant stature. I knew who stood invisibly around us.

"You're correct, sir," I concurred, nodding my head with each word. "I'm not Justine."

"You look like her, but you're not her." A snarl ripped from his lips. "Who are you?"

I narrowed my eyes. "My name is Jenny. I'm Justine's sister."

His eyes widened. "Where is she? Where is Justine?!" He took both hands and grabbed the fence, wildly shaking it. I stood straighter, undeterred by his hissy fit.

"In a safe place," I answered, my chin lifted. "Away from you."

Sorrow softened his face. "I ... I hurt her, didn't I?"

"You sure did. I don't put up with violence. And neither do the authorities."

Police sirens wailed in the distance, signaling that they were on their way. He let go of the fence and backed up, staring at me with accusing eyes. A growl rumbled deep in his chest and his face blushed a deep red.

"You called the police," he bit out through clenched teeth. He looked like he could explode at any moment.

"You attacked someone on our property," I pointed out. "You will have to be punished for your actions."

"I hate you!" he shouted at me, punching at the fence. Spittle clung to the corners of his mouth.

"Pete, you must be careful what you say." I stared him right in the eyes. "In the bible it says that if anyone hates another brother or sister, they are a murderer at heart. And murderers don't have eternal life within them."

Police cars lined the streets, tires squealing and voices shouting. A herd of footsteps pounded the concrete, each step getting closer and closer.

Suddenly he jumped at the fence, taking me by surprise. "If I go to prison, when I get out, I will kill you."

"You can threaten all you want, but the Holy Spirit is on my side." I inched closer to his face. "Don't listen to the voices in your head. They speak death and lies."

"You will pay!" he screamed, showering me with saliva.

Calmly, I wiped my face with the back of my hand. "You need help, Pete. When you get out, come back here. We can help you."

Pete glared at me until the police tackled him to the ground. He fought the whole time, until finally they were able to cuff him. As they led him away he yelled profanities at them, spitting in their faces.

"You can't save him."

I jumped at the deep voice. The robe-wearing demon was back, wearing his hood. He peered at me with glowing red eyes and a deviant smirk on his face.

"You can't save him," he said again. "He was born into darkness. There is no redemption for him."

"Actually, there is no redemption for *you*," I shot back, feeling the Holy Spirit pour through me. His face contorted into rage, my words striking a nerve.

"We will meet again, Prophet. We will meet again." And with his thoughts out, he disappeared.

"I have no doubt," I muttered under my breath.

Sighing, I walked through the garden and prayed. I thanked God for reminding Justine of His existence. I thanked Him for leading me to her side. With everything Justine had gone through, and finally remembering the day she was saved, she would be able to move forward and use her life as a ministry to help others. True, an uphill battle was imminent, but through Jesus Christ she would be able to conquer it.

And I would be with her every step of the way.

Epilogue

Justine (One year later)

I'm a year clean today. The rehab center is holding a celebration honoring my recovery. Honoring my choice to change for the better. Really, though, the celebration isn't about me. It's about God and how He performs miracles using His perfect timing.

At the age of fourteen I was thrown to the streets. For twelve years I rarely held sobriety in my grasp. I sold my body for drugs, camped out in alleyways, and went dumpster diving for food. That had been my life. Notice the *had been* – that's my past life.

Now I have a new life. A life full of hope and love. A life full of light and dreams. I didn't know the plan God had in motion the day Jenny found me, but one thing is endearingly certain – there is definitely a reason He reunited Jenny and I.

God placed me in the rehab facility to renew my life. To make me seek truth. He allowed Pete to be sent so I could remember a time when I was happy, carefree, and trusting. To help me remember a time when I was happy without the help from drugs.

I have rededicated my life to Christ. My heart, my *whole* heart, belongs to Jesus. My faith, my hope, my dreams are through Him. He is the reason I'm here. And yes, there is a reason for my life.

I have forgiveness in my heart. I forgive Ricky for all the horrible things he did to me. I forgive my mother for throwing me out on the streets. I forgive Pete for hooking me on drugs. I forgive anyone that has hurt me in the past. Forgiveness is key to moving on from a hurtful past life.

Along with getting my life in order, God has slowly been giving me insight into the spiritual realm. I have seen things that curl my toes and freeze me with fear; I've also seen things that are so glorious, tears pour down my face because of all the splendor.

Jenny's unfazed by what I see, because she sees them as well. She has seen them before. I like that we see things together. It makes the transition into this whole new world easier on me.

If people could see what we see, they wouldn't soak

themselves in such sinful lifestyles. They wouldn't chase after the world's temporary highs, or have the "If it feels good, do it" mentality. They wouldn't be so quick to do evil. If they could see that the way they're living determines their eternities, they'd run as fast as they could into God's arms.

However, He gave mankind freewill. Sadly many will not find eternal life. Many will perish in the flames of Hell. For all eternity. When we die here on earth, it's not the end. It's the beginning.

I can see that now. Looking back on my life, I had been on the road to Hell and would've ended up being tormented forever. Thankfully God is a gracious and merciful God. His love for His children is endless. I've been reading the Holy Bible, and one of my favorite verses is found in the book of Psalms, chapter eighty-six, verse five:

For you, Lord, are good, and ready to forgive; and plenteous in mercy to all them that call on you.

I called out his name. He answered me. He saved me. And now I will live the rest of my life for Him. I'm living proof that miracles happen. God is an on-time God. His timing is always perfect. Jesus is my stronghold, my fortress. My life is a gift, and I will not waste it.

I've been given a new lease on life, and I will not waste a second of it.

Not. One. Second.

Note From The Author....

Hello readers! I wanted to take this time to thank you for purchasing this series and I hope you are enjoying it. With that said, I wanted to let you in on something ... this won't be the last time you read about the Stancil sisters.

I have to admit, writing this story was difficult. With Eternity being a short story series, I found it hard not to go over the word limit with the sisters. These two could possibly have a series of their own someday. Whatever God wants, I'll do.

However, for now you'll be able to read about them in future stories in this series. They may not appear in all, but in a few.

Again, thank you so much for purchasing the Eternity series. Be on the lookout for more!

God Bless!

Jenna Kay Pridgen

www.ingramcontent.com/pod-product-compliance
Lightning Source LLC
Chambersburg PA
CBHW060423130626
46555CB00005B/2191